SEEING *in the* QUIET

LINDA COTTON JEFFRIES

MILFORD HOUSE

an imprint of Sunbury Press, Inc.
Mechanicsburg, PA USA

MILFORD HOUSE

an imprint of Sunbury Press, Inc.
Mechanicsburg, PA USA

For information about special discounts for bulk purchases, please contact Sunbury Press Orders Dept. at (855) 338-8359 or orders@sunburypress.com.

To request one of our authors for speaking engagements or book signings, please contact Sunbury Press Publicity Dept. at publicity@sunburypress.com.

FIRST MILFORD HOUSE PRESS EDITION: October 2021

Set in Adobe Garamond | Interior design by Crystal Devine | Cover by Alyssa Roth | Edited by Lawrence Knorr.

Publisher's Cataloging-in-Publication Data
Names: Jeffries, Linda Cotton, author.
Title: Seeing in the quiet / Linda Cotton Jeffries.
Description: First trade paperback edition. | Mechanicsburg, PA : Milford House Press, 2021.
Summary: Once, Audrey Markum's keen eye for detail led to the discovery of a child's body and the identity of his killer. Now an adult, that early skill has led her to work as a photographer for weddings *and* the Pittsburgh Police Department. When the wealthy Margot Pelletier is found dead at the bottom of her mansion's staircase, the department must determine if she fell or was pushed. Audrey is eager to help but when the child's killer is released from prison, she finds herself fighting for her life as he attempts to settle the old score.
Identifiers: ISBN : 978-1-62006-580-8 (softcover).
Subjects: FICTION / Mystery & Detective / Women Sleuths | FICTION / Action & Adventure | FICTION / Crime.

Product of the United States of America
0 1 1 2 3 5 8 13 21 34 55

Continue the Enlightenment!

for David

husband, best friend, and ping pong buddy

ACKNOWLEDGMENTS

A number of very special, longtime friends have kept me going through this writing and publishing process. They include many of my early readers as well as my walking companions, Dorothy Ebersole, Jan Weston, and Tina Ezekiel. There is something so special about friends you've known for decades.

I'd like to especially thank the wonderful M. Karen Brawn for her excellent editing advice and insight. Her patience and thoughtful commentary made all the difference!

For their expertise, I'd like to thank my friends Suzanne Biermann M.A, CCC-SLP Speech-Language Pathologist; and Carol Fast MSPA, CCC-SLP, also a Speech-Language Pathologist. Their oversight and knowledge were invaluable. I'd also like to thank Carl Ent, former Chief of Police for Ann Arbor, Michigan, for his expertise in the workings of police investigations and procedures.

As always, I'd like to thank my husband and the rest of my family for their unwavering love and support.

PROLOGUE

"Come, let's dance." A hand fell on her shoulder, the weight familiar and certain. The orchestra was playing a favorite song. Its melody seemed just out of reach, but the rhythm was a gentle one, and they moved easily in each other's arms. They both looked so fine, she thought. She was wearing the dark, jade green dress that she'd saved up for, while her husband looked exceptionally handsome in his new charcoal suit with the thin, tight lapels and widely spaced buttons. He was still clean-shaven, she noted, as the music swelled, and he moved them skillfully around the dance floor to where the higher-ranking attendees were mingling and chatting. It was the first inaugural ball they'd ever attended, and she couldn't get over how elegant the new First Lady looked, her sleeveless dress accented by the long, white gloves. Margot looked down and saw that she too was wearing gloves, the lace backing delicate and a little worn, a gift from her mother after the war. Suddenly her mind filled with two images of her mother, young and vibrant, laughing as she showed off the gloves, then withered and dry as she lay on the deep, blue velvet.

The images were unsettling, but they were driven away when her husband bent over and whispered to her. She couldn't quite hear what he was saying, so she leaned in closer, loving how it felt to hold him again, to be held. She could smell his aftershave and a hint of the starch in his shirt collar, all of it wonderfully familiar. He lifted her gently off her feet for just a moment, and her breath caught with the thrill of it as she seemed to float just above the scene. Then he brought her back down and kissed her behind her ear.

A bright light shown down on the new first couple, and they paused in their dance to clap, but the spotlight moved and began to shine directly into her eyes. She shifted to turn away from it when an ache moved through her hip, and she felt herself struggling to turn over in bed. She came awake suddenly and wanted to weep for the vivid smell and feel of her husband, gone now for so many years. She was angry at her hip and at time and at whatever had conspired to wake her from such a wonderful dream. She opened her eyes. A bright full moon was beaming through her window at her. She watched as the oak trees' branches shifted in front of it, a gentle wind moving and blowing them about. In two weeks, their leaves would have blocked any moonlight and left her to sleep, dreaming in her husband's embrace. If only.

She tried to turn over and fall back into the dream, but her hip continued to ache, and sleep wouldn't return. Finally, she decided to get up and fix herself a cup of tea, something soothing that might let her fall back to sleep. Or maybe she'd carry it out into the moonlit garden if it was warm enough, the way she and Arnaud used to do. She got up stiffly and went to the closet, pulling out the light robe that matched her nightgown. The set was a little worn but still beautiful, she thought, and wished again for those lost moments with her husband. She stepped into the new slippers and walked around the corner to the elevator. She looked down at her feet, thinking that the bows made them look especially silly, but her granddaughter had bought them for her, so she loved them. Of course, her granddaughter had no idea that she never wore slippers, never went downstairs in her dressing gown at all.

She pushed the button a second and third time but with no effect. The thing was probably waiting at the bottom, with its button stuck again. She hated the elevator, or rather the necessity for it, but with bedrooms all the way up on the third floor, there had been no other choice. At least twenty years old now, it was due to be replaced. Having it installed was one of the last things her husband had done, preparing the house for them to grow old in together. The gap between their ages had never bothered her until old age had come for them both and taken him away first. She shook her head and began heading to the stairs. It wasn't fair that he couldn't be there with her now. It just wasn't. She held onto the rail carefully as she stepped down to the second floor then around the curve of the atrium. As she moved forward, she looked up at the high windows, studying the full moon that had filled her window and awakened her from the lovely dream. In that instant, her feet were out from under her, and she was falling and falling.

"Arnaud!" She screamed.

CHAPTER

1

Twenty years earlier

"Mom!" Audrey wailed as the video screen disappeared into blackness, her finger mashing on the button that would have carried her up to the next level.

She looked up to see her mother standing and glaring at her, hands planted on her hips. "You're not listening to me! I told you half a dozen times to turn that game off. We have to get ready. Your dad's already on his way back from the airport."

Audrey slammed the controller on the sofa and stomped down the hallway to her room. The awful black dress was laid out on her bed, so she threw her pajamas off and pulled it on over her head. She headed to her mother's room for her to do the zipper in the back for her, then climbed up onto the wide bed behind her to wait. Audrey watched as her mother's bottom settled onto the worn vanity bench, its cloth raveling at the edges after years of use. Above the table perched an old mirror, the ornate wooden edges painted white in some previous existence well before the yard sale where her mother had found it. Dust lay in each of the wooden curls, and Audrey watched as an ant meandered up the long, winding side. She studied its progress intently, focusing as each tiny leg lifted up over the gritty mounds that clung to the individual whorls of the design. Her mother was speaking to her, but Audrey hadn't realized it until the ant managed to make it to the top of the mirror and disappear.

Hours later, sometime after the minister left the room, Audrey slipped off her shoes. They were a little small, the shiny black strap cutting the top of her foot in an arc that she knew would be mirrored in a red mark on the skin beneath the dark socks. She was sitting in an overstuffed armchair. Her legs were too short to reach the floor, so they swung back and forth in a rhythm that matched the slow voices around her. There was a sick, flowery smell to the room that Audrey hated, and she wiggled in the dress until she was able to pull the front of it up over her nose. Her breath was warm and smelled faintly of Frosted Flakes, a big improvement over the flowers, she thought. Audrey knew very few of the adults who stood scattered around the big funeral parlor, but she watched their faces closely. It kept her eyes from traveling across the room to where the casket lid was propped open, and her grandfather lay so still.

With one hand still holding up the collar of her dress, she reached into her pocket with the other and fingered a thin, brown hairpin that she'd found on the floor earlier. It was one of her mother's, the kind with the open U shape, wavy on each side. She remembered the moment that morning when her mother had tucked it into a bun at the back of her head, her right hand tilted as she maneuvered it around a loop of hair that was threatening to come loose. Audrey hated when her mother pulled her hair back like that, preferring the long, gentle sweep that sometimes tickled her nose as she hugged her mother before leaving for school each morning. This morning, though, all of the soft bits had been pulled back into a tight collection that she sprayed again and again with the awful, artificial scent that filled the air around them. Audrey sneezed and then held her breath until she finished. Her mother replaced the can on the back of the table and let her arms fall to her sides as if the preparations had exhausted her. She looked at Audrey's image in the mirror and managed a sort of half-smile, but it quickly dimmed, and she stood up reluctantly, tucking a tissue into a pocket with one hand while reaching out for Audrey's hand with the other.

Although she could picture that morning's scene easily, even the ant climbing on the mirror, Audrey remembered nothing of what her mother had said. For some reason, Audrey always seemed to see things better than she heard them, her eyes easily catching and holding onto the smallest details while her ears drifted in and out of the world around her. She remembered how her teacher had held her pen in a tight, white-knuckled grip as she talked recently with Audrey's parents about her school performance, describing Audrey's lack of attention to the flow of ideas and events that traveled through the classroom each day. Luckily, now that she was in the third grade, more and more of her work was written down, requiring her to read rather than listen. Reading something was so much easier than listening to someone go on and on.

Today though, there was nothing to read or write, nothing to stop the various adults from pausing and talking at her, their hands touching her hair, her shoulder, the back of the itchy, black dress. When she saw another group approaching, she let the dress front drop and used her arms to push against the armrests, forcing herself further back into the chair, away from those hands that meant well but felt bad. Happily, they walked on by her. Audrey studied her feet out in front of her now, the thin black ankle socks with the white stitching around the scalloped edge. She straightened the toe of one, then put her feet back out in front of her, waiting and watching for the last few people to wander back out the door. Once everyone had left, Audrey saw her parents come into the room behind the man from the funeral parlor. She got down and forced her shoes back on, then walked over to her father and held his hand. Audrey watched as her mother drew a photograph out of her pocket. She tucked it under Audrey's grandfather's hands next to his heart and stepped back before nodding to the man. Just before he lowered the lid, he bowed his head briefly, and Audrey dropped the hairpin inside.

2

Audrey sat in the wide plastic chair next to her mother, eyeing the pile of toys scattered in the corner of the waiting room. They were the kind you saw in every waiting room, wires with beads that went nowhere, building blocks in various colors, their edges all gray from use, dolls lying on top of the bin, their hair and dresses an unmovable plastic. An old-fashioned metal-looking pail held dozens of small cars and trucks. Audrey could picture herself lining the cars up in a tight row or setting up an obstacle course with the blocks, but instead, she sat, waiting nervously, sure that she was going to fail whatever test they were heading toward. Her stomach growled, and she pushed her hands against her middle just as her mother reached a soft-sweatered arm around her shoulders.

"It's going to be okay, Audrey, I promise." But Audrey wasn't sure. How could not hearing be okay? She had watched the conversation between her parents at the dinner table the night after the parent-teacher conference, the tension around their eyes, the way a dish being passed would pause in mid-air, hovering while one of them spoke. They didn't seem to be angry with her, but it was hard to tell exactly how they felt. Her father talked about how expensive it might be, while her mother shook her head repeatedly, insisting that she didn't care what it cost. Finally, after an especially long exchange, they seemed to remember that Audrey was sitting right there with them at the table, her fork shaking slightly in her hand. Her father gave her a lopsided kind of smile and returned to the food in front of him, while her mother dabbed at her mouth with a napkin and then leaned closer to ask Audrey about her school day. It was such an odd dinner. She was relieved when her father pushed his chair back and began clearing dishes, the signal that she was finally free to go.

Back in her room that evening, Audrey sat on the floor at the end of her bed. She turned on her CD player and alternated between placing her hand over one ear, then the other, and then both. She thought that her hearing seemed pretty good that night. She could definitely tell a big difference in the music when she muffled and unmuffled her ears, but of course, she was trying hard to listen. She knew that she was happy just to let sounds wash over her a lot of times while studying something with her eyes. It felt like sometimes she learned much more that way.

Just that morning, a boy in her class named Toby had had a birthday, and after they'd sung for him, his mother had brought out a big plastic container filled with fancy cupcakes. The icing was piled in neat swirls of blue and white, every one of them topped with a bright, candy Nemo. Audrey watched as his mother handed each child a napkin, and then Toby handed around the cupcakes. But it seemed to her that Toby's eyes didn't look quite right, certainly not the way you'd expect someone to look on their birthday. She noticed too that his mother kept pulling the neckline of her shirt tighter, the gaping edge of it revealing a bright pink line along her throat. Audrey looked at Toby again as he reached out and back, his sleeve sliding back and forth on his small wrist where purple and red spots made an angry-looking circle. Audrey listened carefully to the talk around her, but no one seemed to notice how strange Toby and his mom seemed or say anything about it. The air just filled with sounds that didn't matter, the same comments that people made every time there was a birthday and treats.

When the nurse came out to announce their turn, Audrey took her mother's hand and followed her into the doctor's office. It was bigger than she expected with a long counter on one side with a strange-looking computer. She watched as her mother talked with the doctor, telling her about Audrey's allergies and ear infections. The doctor seemed to nod a lot and make notes on a tall clipboard that she set across her knees. Audrey did her best to focus on the doctor and hear what was being said. She nodded as her mother talked and waited for the moment when the doctor would zero in on her. It didn't take long. Soon she was seated in front of the strange machine while the doctor poked a kind of headphone into her ear and rested something else on her shoulder. Later on, the doctor had her close her eyes and raise her hand each time she heard a sound. Sometimes she thought she heard something but wasn't sure. At other times, it all seemed to go very still and quiet. She sneaked one eye open to see if the doctor was still there just as Dr. Barnes looked up from her machine. Audrey quickly shut her eyes, embarrassed that she'd been caught peeking.

Finally, the doctor finished and went to the door to bring Audrey's mother back in. "The good news is that there doesn't seem to be any infection at the moment. However, there does appear to be fluid in both ears right now, as well as some diminished hearing on both sides. Given the number of infections, I'd like us to try putting in some tubes so that we can drain the fluid and see if that makes a difference in her hearing." Audrey gulped. That sounded terrible to her. Tubes? Like test tubes? How would that work? Really, she could just work harder at paying attention, she thought. But her mother nodded and made an appointment for later that week. In bed that night, Audrey pulled her old stuffed dog a little closer, rubbing his soft ears against her cheek as she worried about having an operation. Her dad came and sat on the side of her bed, trying to reassure her about everything, but when the door closed behind him, her fears grew big again, and she tucked herself into a tight ball as she waited for sleep.

The next day she returned to school and tried her best to follow what the teacher and her classmates said. It was tiring, though, and really, she just wanted to read and draw and study the spider that was building a web across the window by her desk. She watched as he pulled each line straight and tight, moving slowly around the window frame doing his careful work. By Thursday morning, it was a thing of beauty, perfectly formed. It hovered just above the window, a few drops of dew caught on the lowest strands. That afternoon when she returned to her seat after lunch, she went to look and see if he'd caught anything in his beautiful web, but someone had opened the window, tilting it wide as the spring sun grew warmer. The torn edges of the web waved in the breeze as the air moved into the classroom, but the careful spider was nowhere to be seen. Audrey went back to her seat, rested her chin on her desk, and waited for the school day to end.

Friday morning, instead of going to school, her mother and father took her to a clinic at the hospital. She was frightened as they walked in, icky smells filling the cool air and adding to her fears. She was wearing her best pajamas with her school shoes, and that seemed wrong and a little embarrassing. She wondered if people thought she didn't know how to get dressed in the morning. Before long, they followed a tall, thin man into a space with a bed that had curtains all around it. She took off her shoes, and they tucked her under a shiny white sheet and a blanket that had been warmed somehow. It felt nice, she thought, as they gave her a dose of medicine that smelled of cherries but tasted sharper and hotter. She let the sound of her parents' voices wash over her as she fell asleep.

"Wake up, sleepyhead." Her dad pulled on her pinky finger, and Audrey felt herself coming awake slowly, the lines of her father's face fuzzy and unclear for a moment before she finally reached the surface. She couldn't believe it was over already. She touched her hands to her ears, afraid that she would feel the tubes sticking out, making her look like a freak of some kind. But all she felt was a bit of cotton in each ear and an achiness inside. Her father and mother were smiling at her. They looked happy, she thought, and wondered if maybe they had been a little bit afraid, too. Her mom helped her sit up and gave her some cereal with a banana cut up in it. Then the three of them played a long game of cards. Finally, Dr. Barnes appeared and removed the cotton, placing a few drops of some liquid in each ear. After that, her dad picked her up and carried her down the hall. Audrey's head swiveled back and forth as she listened to the sounds of the hospital. A quiet whooshing came out of one room, a steady beeping out of another, and a loud clang sounded at the end of the hallway when a metal cart crashed into the edge of a vending machine.

In the car, her father opened the windows to cool it off, and she could hear the wind as it rushed past her. The engine made a sound that she could feel through her pajama bottoms. She rested her hand on the seat, matching what she'd felt many times before with what she could now hear. An ambulance came toward them suddenly, its siren screaming as it slowed beside them before turning a corner. Audrey clapped her hands over her ears, wishing she still had some of the cotton from the hospital. But finally, the noise began to diminish, and her father clicked on the radio. Someone was talking at first, but he pushed the buttons until he found a station playing the kind of jazz he liked. Audrey eased back in the seat, watching and listening as they sped toward home.

By Monday morning, the pain had gone away, and she was growing used to hearing the world around her a little more clearly. She liked listening to the music that her dad played and the pop music that her mother switched to once he'd gone off to do something else. The cartoons that she watched on TV seemed to make a little more sense to her, but she still didn't feel like watching them for very long. She hated the sound that the coffee grinder made as one last bean whirled round and round in the hopper, and the alarm clock nearly scared her to death when it buzzed in the dark on Monday morning.

That morning she dressed carefully in her favorite pants and striped blue shirt and put her stuffed dog back up on the shelf. She watched as the syrup filled in each square dent of her waffle before cutting it apart and putting the units into her mouth carefully, one by one. The bus to school seemed to roar beneath her, the gears grinding loudly into place, the brakes squealing as they came to each stop. In the classroom, she could hear the fish tanks bubbling on the back table and the mean tone in a boy's voice when he made fun of Toby's torn jeans. She heard Toby laugh off the remark, but she watched his face and knew that it had hurt. She thought she saw a scrape through the torn material on his knee and was about to ask him about it when the teacher came in and started the morning's routine.

By the time the school bus let her off in front of her house that afternoon, Audrey was exhausted. She waved to her mom in the kitchen but didn't stop, heading straight to her bedroom. She lifted her stuffed dog back off the shelf and lay down on the bed, pulling her pillow over her ears. She was asleep in minutes.

"There, shut off that light." The darkness returned quickly, and it was a few seconds before the man's eyes adjusted once again. He tamped the dirt down hard with the back of the shovel before handing it to his wife. Then he picked up the lightweight rake and took his time scattering dry leaves and small branches over the entire area. In the near darkness, he studied the look of it carefully before handing the rake to her. He exchanged it for the light, which he turned on its lowest setting for a brief moment as he checked over the area. Once he was sure of his bearings, he shut it off and tucked it into his waistband before taking up the handles of the wheelbarrow.

He barked at her once more. "Stop that damned sniveling. I've had enough." They were through the small stand of woods and back at the house in just a few minutes. She turned to go inside while he continued through their darkened backyard to the lot behind theirs, where he returned the wheelbarrow. A lawn care company was installing a sprinkler system and would never know it had been gone. He propped the shovel up against the shed with all of their other tools and returned, picking his way through the blackness, to his own yard. He pulled off the work gloves and tossed them in the garbage can before carrying it down and setting it on the curb for the morning pickup. The gloves had been next to useless anyway, he thought, as he rubbed the palm of his hand, now worn raw and sore. Coming back up the short slope, he stumbled over the rake but managed not to fall. His lazy bitch of a wife must have dropped it on the grass. He went and clipped it carefully into place on the inside wall of the garage and then went inside to deal with her.

CHAPTER

4

Three weeks later, Audrey was growing more used to the new sounds in her world. The end of school was getting closer, and the days were filled with final projects and activities, even a field trip to the downtown museum. After dinner one evening, she sat curled beside her father on the sofa while he watched the evening news and flicked absently through a golf magazine. Suddenly she looked up, recognizing the name from her classroom. She looked at her father, and the two of them leaned a little closer as the announcer spoke.

"Their son missing now for more than twenty-four hours, young Toby Adams's parents have grown frantic. They are reaching out to the community this evening for help." The camera switched to a couple standing in front of a house, the man talking in a loud voice while the woman stood beside him with tears coming down her face. Audrey recognized Toby's mother and, although she'd never been inside, she knew the house from her bus route. The man was pleading for people to help set up search parties before Audrey's dad muted the television and called out to her mother. Audrey could hear him on the phone, offering to join in the search. She continued to watch the silent scene on the television as flashbulbs glared and faded one after the other. She studied Toby's father's face, looking for the sadness she knew would cover her father's face in the same situation. It didn't look right, though. It was the eyes, she thought, and something about the edges of his mouth that didn't look sad or worried. Instead, they looked angry and a little bit mean, she thought. She felt terrible that she hadn't noticed Toby missing from her classroom at school.

That Sunday night at dinner, Audrey saw how tired her dad looked. He had been on the search team for three days, and they had found nothing. Their development was bordered by a stand of woods with a stream through it on one side and the highway on the other side. By now, they had gone through the woods several times and had begun searching the water with a specialized crew. "They've called off the teams for now," he said as he rested his hand on the table after taking just a few bites. "The current thinking is that probably someone took him. They could be two or three states away by now."

"Why would someone take a boy?" Audrey asked. Her father turned and put his hand on top of hers.

"There's no way to know, honey, but I want you to be extra careful when you're coming home." She saw him look back at her mother, the two of them clearly nervous about the subject.

"It's just the bus, Dad. Toby quit riding the bus."

Her mother tilted her head as she looked at Audrey. "When did he stop riding the bus? It goes right past their house."

Audrey shrugged, "I can't remember. Sometime after his birthday."

"Did his mother drive him every morning?" She set the tongs back in the salad bowl without taking any.

Audrey shook her head. "No, his dad drove. Toby sat in the backseat with his mom." She saw her parents look at one another again, but nothing more was said.

Weeks later, the final day of school arrived, and Audrey jumped off the bus with sticky hands and the last bits of her ice cream, threatening to run out the bottom of the cone. She stuffed one final, cold bite into her mouth and waved back at her friend Sandy as the bus pulled away from the curb. Town kids sometimes made fun of the bus riders, but Audrey knew that no one took *them* out for ice cream on the way home the way their driver did at the end of school each June.

Although she'd done well in school that year, better after she'd gotten the tubes in her ears, Audrey was still thrilled to see it end. She loved her neighborhood and the freedom that summer gave her and her friends. Since her mother and father both worked, Audrey spent each weekday at Sandy's house. It was a plan that their parents had worked out the year before, and she loved it. Sandy's house was much closer to the neighborhood pool than hers, so they usually divided their time between the two places. Audrey knew that many of the kids from her class would probably spend their summer playing video games or watching TV, but she and Sandy weren't like that. For one thing, their parents were in strict agreement about setting limits on screen times. Sandy's mom especially made them "earn" it by logging time outdoors. Last summer, Toby hadn't been allowed to play video games either, so the three of them had spent a lot of time riding bikes and playing together outside in the woods or around the neighborhood.

The first morning of summer, she and Sandy started the day by heading to the top of Snake Hill. To Audrey, it felt as though the sun's heat was sinking right into her skin, not glancing off the way it did in spring. Summer was finally here, and biking up and then flying down the long twisting hill felt like the perfect beginning to it. If only Toby had been there to enjoy it with them.

After half a dozen trips left them feeling exhausted, she and Sandy rode slowly around the flatter streets until they caught their breath. Sandy was practicing riding without her hands, but Audrey was a little too afraid to try that. Instead, she swung her legs out wide and deliberately wove the bike back and forth in a meandering path. Then they rode slowly, side by side, past Toby's house.

"I miss having Toby to play with," Sandy mentioned as she lined up even with Audrey.

"Me too. Do you think somebody took him somewhere?"

"I don't know. Where would somebody take him? And why?"

"I don't know. It's just what my dad keeps saying. I think he's a little scared in case someone comes back to the neighborhood and wants to take someone else. Are you scared?"

Sandy shrugged. "Not really. My mom and dad haven't said much about it, but my brothers and I are supposed to check in more often. I guess we'd better go and do that."

They rode together around the quiet streets before turning into Sandy's driveway and dropping their bikes onto her front lawn. Audrey loved staying at Sandy's house. It was so much more interesting than her own.

With three brothers, a dog, and a cat, it seemed to be filled with activity and noise. Secretly, she thought Sandy's mom, Cecelia Wilder, was a little bit crazy too, but in a good way. She had an art studio in the back of their house and wore paint-covered smocks over wide, flowing skirts. Her long black hair was always piled up on the top of her head with a pencil or pen somehow holding it in place.

"Mom," Sandy yelled toward the back of the house as she pulled the freezer door open. She handed Audrey a bright green freezer-pop and took a purple one for herself. Then she slammed the door shut and snipped off the tops of the wrappers. She dropped the sticky scissors on the counter and yelled out again as they walked back toward the studio. "We're here!"

Audrey followed Sandy down the back steps and out to the studio. Once, it had been a kind of shed attached to the side of a regular garage, but sometime in the past, it had grown to take over the entire space. Stacked haphazardly around the room, it looked to Audrey as though the canvases Mrs. Wilder painted had grown even larger than she remembered. She had filled them with bright colors and thick gobs of paint that Audrey didn't understand. None of them looked like anything she could recognize, but there was a kind of excitement to the images that she liked. A dark, wooden fan that was speckled and dusty hung from the ceiling, slowly stirring the scents of paint and turpentine that she always associated with Sandy's mom. She sucked on the cold ice-pop as they talked.

"Have you girls been having fun?" Mrs. Wilder stirred a brush into a tall jar, and Audrey watched as the bright color swirled for a moment before mixing into the brown.

"We've been riding bikes. Where are the boys?"

"They wanted to go to the pool, so they're putting on their suits. Do you girls want to go, too?"

Sandy looked at Audrey but knew the answer already. "Of course!"

"All right, go and get ready, and I'll walk all of you over there. By the way, I talked to your mom this morning, Audrey. She's glad that you girls are checking in with me. She dropped off your suit on her way to the clinic." Both girls grinned and slapped hands before heading back toward the house to get some food and change their clothes.

The first day at the pool had been terrific, even though Audrey had gotten a little bit of sunburn on her shoulders. But it was three days later before the rain stopped, and they were able to get back outside. Sandy's house was pretty fun, and they'd kept busy building blanket forts and baking cookies. Sandy's mother had even set them up with real paints in her studio, but they were eager to get back outside today. At last, they were back on their bikes, cruising around the neighborhood. Audrey had been thinking about Toby a lot while they were playing inside. "Remember how Toby was always talking about us building a tree fort this summer? He told us he'd found a spot in the woods where three trees stood close together."

"Why don't we go and see if we can find it?" Sandy asked. "We can build just as good as a boy can. My dad even has wood leftover from when he fixed our back porch. It's just sitting in a pile, making my mom mad. My brothers could help us carry it."

They rode back to Sandy's house and filled an old backpack with water and snacks before grabbing a plastic baggie that held chunky sidewalk chalk. The woods weren't dense, and they knew them pretty well, but they figured that once they found the three trees, they could mark a clear path back to the house. That way, it would be easy to bring in the wood and supplies that they would need to build.

Neither of them had figured on it being quite so muddy, though. They left their bikes at the edge of the woods and then walked single file along an old path. It was rough with tree roots and stones sticking up and places where the rain had left deep pockets of mud. They had to go slowly, watching for the trees that Toby had mentioned and being careful that they didn't lose a flip-flop to the sticky mud. The path petered out after about twenty yards, and they stood back-to-back looking around them, trying to decide which direction Toby might have gone.

"Let's go that way." Audrey pointed to the left. The light was stronger in that direction, and she had a sense that if you kept going straight through, you'd end up back on Toby's street. He might have come in from that direction. The rocky clearing that they all liked to climb on was in that direction as well.

There were limestone rocks and outcroppings all over the area, even caves in some places, they had heard. This spot, where the trees opened up and sunlight was able to enter, included a horseshoe-shaped pile of rock. Some were flat, low to the ground, and slick with the recent rains, but near the middle, others were stacked one on top of the other and reached well over their heads. Audrey and Sandy climbed up onto the lowest slab, then inched their way forward and up onto the taller, more rugged sections. From there, they could see a little way into the woods, and Audrey thought that she might have spotted the three trees that they were looking for. All around them, the rain had washed deep gullies, some now starting to fill with wildflowers, while others were clogged with last autumn's leaves. They jumped down, and Sandy wandered off to the left, but something bright had caught Audrey's eye. She thought at first that it was just a colorful wildflower that they hadn't seen before, but as she drew closer, its shape and color grew more distinct. It was crescent-shaped and a shade of orange that nature hadn't made. She knelt beside it, and the air around her grew still and silent. She couldn't hear Sandy or the birds, only the beating of her own heart. She knew what it was without touching it, the edge of a tennis shoe.

Without speaking, Audrey reached into their bag and drew out a bright blue piece of sidewalk chalk. She scratched a wide 'X' across the width of the nearest tree, then pocketed the chalk and took off running. She found Sandy looking up at the trees around her, pointing at a group of three that were perfectly spaced for making a triangular fort, but Audrey yelled "c'mon!" and grabbed her by the elbow, pulling her back toward the rocks and their path home.

When Sandy balked, Audrey dropped her arm and ran on ahead. "What's going on?" her friend called as Audrey rushed to where they'd left their bikes. But Audrey didn't want to explain. She just wanted to get home. She yelled back something about a chore she'd forgotten to do, leapt onto her bike, and took off for home, pedaling as quickly as she could. She tossed her bike onto the grass by the front walk and tore inside. Audrey knew her father was getting over a bad cold and working from home that morning. She was racing for his study when she saw him standing in the kitchen, his hand on the refrigerator door.

Her breath was ragged, and the fear that had swept over her at first came rushing back. She threw herself at him and buried her face in the soft cotton of his old t-shirt. "Audie, what's going on, honey? What's wrong?"

She held on to his middle but turned her head so that she could speak. It came out as a whisper, "A shoe, Daddy, I saw a shoe."

"Why would you be so scared of a shoe, honey? Weren't you over at Sandy's house?" He closed the refrigerator and walked her over to the kitchen table, settling her in the seat and then kneeling in front of her. "I don't understand."

"It's in the woods. We went looking for a place to build a tree fort, and I saw it in the woods, not far from all the rocks."

"I still don't understand. Somebody probably just lost a shoe when they were out hiking. That doesn't seem like a big deal to me."

It was hard for Audrey to explain. Somehow she knew it wasn't just a lost shoe. A lost shoe would have been left on its side, maybe filled with mud or leaves or something. Plus, she had recognized the bright orange design. "It's Toby's, Daddy. I know it is."

Audrey's father grew still. He rested his hands on the sides of her chair before reaching to smooth her hair back behind her ears. Audrey could see that he believed her, and, suddenly, she felt even more scared because his face now looked scared as well. "I'm going to make a call, honey, then will you show me where you found it?" Audrey nodded and sat very still as he went to use the phone.

When the police car arrived, it wasn't using its lights or siren, but Audrey was still afraid to get in. Her father held onto her hand, coaxing her into the backseat and then sitting beside her. She told him the route they had taken from Sandy's house to the entrance to the woods. The police car drove slowly through the neighborhood, around the corner to her friend's house, and then beyond it to the opening into the woods. As they passed by, Audrey was relieved to see that her friend's bike was back at home. How in the world would she ever explain what had happened to Sandy?

Although she knew she was too big for it, when they stepped out of the car, her father picked her up in his arms and asked her quietly to point the way. They went first, with the policeman following behind. She could hear sudden bursts of sound from the radio hooked on his shoulder, but there was nothing that she could understand. When the path ended, they turned again and headed toward the outcropping of rocks. Audrey's father set her down on one of the higher ones, and she pointed off to her right.

"Can you see it, Daddy, there between the trees?" When he shook his head in confusion, Audrey climbed down and took his hand. "It's just up here a little way. I put a big 'X' on the tree next to it."

When they were close enough to see the 'X,' the policeman held out his arm to stop them. Audrey watched as the man stepped forward carefully and then crouched on the ground. He reached out with a pen and dug gently around the part of the shoe that she'd seen. Then he stopped and leaned his head to the side, talking rapidly into the radio. He stood up and then walked back to speak to Audrey and her father. "Did you touch anything, Audrey, when you came here before?" The policeman bent over slightly in front of her. She watched his face but couldn't tell what he was thinking.

"No, I was too scared. I just ran home and told my dad."

"Is it . . . ?" Her father started to ask, but the policeman gave one quick nod and turned his head. Audrey's father bent down and pulled her into a close hug. "You did a good job, honey. We're going to go back out to the street now and let some other policemen come in and look around."

They retraced their steps, and by the time they reached the edge of the woods, the air had filled with the sound of sirens. Audrey put her hands over her ears and let her father lead her back to the car they'd ridden in. Ears covered, she watched as men and women climbed out of three other police cars, opening trunks and taking out shovels and rakes. She noticed one man had a large camera around his neck and wondered what that might be for. A little later on, an ambulance pulled up behind the police cars, but it didn't have its lights on or its siren.

As Audrey looked around her at the line of people moving about, in and out of the woods, she noticed one more police car go slowly past them in the opposite direction. It looked as if two people were sitting in the backseat of it, one with their head bowed completely, but the other person was looking straight out the window at her. It was Toby's dad, and as she watched, his eyes locked onto hers and stared.

CHAPTER

5

Breakfast was just the way he liked it, the eggs perfectly round and the bacon lying in four crisp parallel lines across the white plate. He used his knife and fork to cut the bacon in half and the toast, then each egg. When the pieces were all ready, he made four neat stacks and proceeded to eat them one by one. A newscast was playing on the small television set over the sink, but he paid it little attention. After all, it seemed as though most of the bullshit was finally over. The back of his mind registered sports scores, pool openings, and a start to a mayoral race, but there was nothing else of interest. Just the way he liked it.

His wife was standing hunch-shouldered at the sink scrubbing something, but he ignored that as well. At least she was quiet. Once finished, he pushed back his chair and left to use the bathroom. He pissed and flushed and then squeezed the styling gel into his hand and worked it into his hair carefully before combing it out just right. At the office, he knew there were women who talked about him, he'd heard them as he entered the lunchroom, and he could tell that they were interested. But lately, just when he thought he could stop the play-acting, maybe give the blonde a special look, he'd hear the whispered comments and have to put his grieving father face back into place. It was exhausting.

He turned off the light and fan and opened the bathroom door just as his wife was about to knock. Her fist hung in the air, and he was about to backhand her out of his way when a policeman entered the space.

"Gary, I . . ." His wife started to speak, but the officer was quicker.

"Mr. Adams, Mrs. Adams, we need you to come with us."

He said nothing to anyone, just climbed into the police cruiser's back seat as they were directed. He couldn't even look at his wife. It was so disgusting. She was bawling again, strings of her hair caught in the snot and tears until he wanted to puke. Instead, he locked his gaze on the outside, on the miserable little neighborhood where he'd stupidly thought he could be happy. As they passed the police cars lining the side of the road, he caught sight of a young girl looking out the window of one, and somehow, he knew. It was her fault. He stared, knowing he would never forget that face.

The next morning, Audrey was glad to find that both of her parents were staying home from work. They sat down together at the breakfast table, a stack of fresh pancakes in the center of the table. Her mother set three small ones on her plate. They weren't in the Mickey Mouse shape that she liked, but something told her it wasn't that sort of a morning. Once they were all seated, she watched as her father took a long drink from his coffee mug and then set it carefully beside his plate. She worried suddenly if she was in trouble for something. At last, he spoke.

"Audrey, we're sad to have to tell you this" Audrey waited, watching the syrup drip ever so slowly from the edge of the bite that she had speared with her fork. Then, as the drop finally reached the plate, he spoke again. "The shoe that you found was Toby's, but the really sad thing is that he didn't lose it in the woods."

Audrey looked up at him and over to her mother, "He was still wearing it, wasn't he?" Her mother nodded. "That's why I didn't touch it, why I was afraid." She set her fork on the edge of her plate and leaned back in her chair. She didn't know what else to say.

"Honey," her mother asked quietly. "Did you ever notice anything wrong with Toby?"

"You mean like at his birthday when his mom brought the cupcakes?" She saw her mother look at her father before turning back to her.

"What makes you ask that?"

Audrey shrugged. "He seemed sad for someone having a birthday. The cupcakes were really pretty, and they tasted good, but he and his mom didn't seem to like them. And she kept trying to hold her shirt closed so you couldn't see the mark around her neck."

Audrey's mother leaned forward. "What kind of mark?"

She closed her eyes for a moment and tried to remember exactly what she'd seen. "It was like she'd had a necklace on that was way too tight, I guess."

"And Toby?" her father asked.

Again Audrey tried her best to see what she remembered from that morning. "Toby's eyes were kind of sad looking, and he'd hurt his arm."

"How do you know that?"

"When he handed us our cupcakes, you could see these marks under his shirt sleeve." She made a circle around her wrist with her thumb and pointer finger. "Right here, like this."

"Aw, Mitch." Audrey's mom turned to her dad and reached out her hand to take his. They both squeezed, and she thought that her mother might have had tears in her eyes.

"Is something wrong? Did I do something wrong?" Audrey asked again, looking from face to face. Her mother got up to get a tissue from the kitchen counter, and her father turned his chair to face her.

"No, you didn't do anything wrong. Come here, Pumpkin."

Audrey climbed into her father's lap, and his arms came around her. She could smell the soap he used and spied a few whiskers he'd missed with his razor. Her mother came back into the room and knelt beside her father's chair as he spoke quietly and carefully. "Toby had been hurt, badly, before he died. Someone choked him until he couldn't breathe anymore. Then they buried him in the woods. We looked all over the woods when he was first lost, but it wasn't until . . ."

"The rain, it was the rain, wasn't it?" Audrey asked, and her father nodded.

"I think we're going to need you to talk to the police again, Audie. They need to know what you saw."

Audrey climbed down from her father's lap and got back into her chair. She picked up the bite of pancake again and put it in her mouth, but it had gotten cold, and the syrup stuck to her fork. Her father went into the other room to use the telephone while her mother poured herself some more coffee and sat back down at the table. The pancakes sat untouched on all three plates.

A little while later, once the table had been cleared and the dishwasher started, Audrey heard voices at the front door. A policewoman in a dark blue uniform came in and sat on the edge of the sofa. She smiled at Audrey and held out her hand for her to shake.

"It's good to meet you, Audrey," she began. Audrey shook the woman's hand briefly and sat down in the armchair across from her. "Your parents told me that you had a little more information for us about your friend Toby. Can you tell me what you remember?"

The conversation didn't last long, but Audrey noticed that the woman seemed to ask the same questions over and over again. It was a little boring. Finally, the policewoman closed the small notebook she had and looked at Audrey with eyes that seemed a little bit tired. Her father led the woman out, but Audrey watched him stop and hold on to the doorframe as they finished talking. She thought that she might have heard the word trial. She went into the kitchen, poured herself a bowl of cereal, and took it to her room. She wasn't supposed to have food in there, but she didn't think her parents would mind today.

Later that summer, Audrey noticed that her left ear kept itching, and she woke up one morning and found a tiny piece of plastic on her pillow. Dr. Barnes had said that the tubes would fall out on their own, so Audrey thought little of it. She put it in the drawer of her nightstand and forgot about it. The world around her grew quieter as it seemed to do every fall when her allergies flared up. She took the allergy medicine that her mother gave her each morning, and although it definitely helped her nose, it seemed to do little for her hearing. She worried that maybe it was even a little worse. There was too much going on, though, to pay it a whole lot of attention.

Toby's dad was going to have a trial. Her parents talked about it all the time, although they usually stopped or dropped their voices when she came into the room. Instead of the end of summer vacation that they'd planned, the police had told them that they had to be close by in case Audrey was called to testify. Audrey wasn't sure exactly what that meant, but she could tell that her parents were trying to do whatever they could to stop it from happening. Finally, the Friday before school started, they got the call.

Audrey's mother helped her put on her best dress, zipping it up for her the way she had for the funeral.

"It's a little tighter than it was, isn't it?"

"I can't get these on either."

Audrey's mother looked at the shoes that Audrey had in her hand and shook her head. "That's not surprising. Oh well." Audrey's mother hugged her tight and kissed her on the cheek. "Sneakers it is then!"

Once Audrey's father had parked the car, they walked hand in hand down the wide sidewalk, Audrey jumping from side to side to avoid the metal grates as they went. They didn't go into the city very often, so she was interested, looking at the cars and streetlights and up around her at the tall office buildings until a huge, stone building loomed in front of them. It was made from enormous, rough blocks of stone. Audrey stopped, reached over to touch one, and looked at both of her parents.

"We have to go in there? This looks like the castle from *Beauty and the Beast* or something. It's so dark! And look, there's a fountain just like the Beast had. Are you sure this is the right place?"

Audrey's dad laughed and looked over her head at her mother. "I guess it is pretty intimidating. Those old builders didn't mess around, did they? Come on, kiddo. No one's going to cast a spell on you."

Audrey was relieved that once they got inside, it looked like just a normal building. They were directed to a bench in a hallway where they sat close together. A few minutes later, a dark, heavyset man came up to them and asked them to follow him, but rather than going into the courtroom as Audrey had seen on TV, they went instead into a sort of big office. A tall woman in a black robe came in, took the robe off and hung it on a hook, and then settled into a wooden chair behind a wide desk. A half-circle of smaller chairs spread around in front of the desk, and Audrey was directed to sit in the center one. Her parents sat on either side of her, and two men she didn't know sat on each end.

The woman took a drink of water and turned to Audrey. She had a nice sort of face with wide cheeks and very white teeth. Her skin was a pretty, dark brown, and her eyes were a flecked green that matched the shirt that she was wearing. "Audrey, I'm Judge Rosen. How are you today?"

"I'm fine," Audrey spoke, but it came out sounding more like a squeak.

"There's no need to worry, now. My assistant is going to record this, and we're just going to have a chat here and decide what to do next." She nodded at a young man sitting at a nearby table, then turned back to face Audrey. "Can you tell me what happened this summer and what you remember from before about your friend, Toby?"

Audrey thought that the room seemed more than silent as if everything around her had stopped or slowed down somehow. She took a deep breath, tucked her hands under her legs, and told her story one more time. She'd lost track of how many times she'd had to repeat it, but the Judge listened quietly without interrupting her. When she finished, the Judge thanked her and then looked around at the adults spread out in front of her.

"Questions, anyone?" When the room remained silent, the judge turned to the man on the left end of their row of chairs. "I take it Mrs. Adams will be testifying this afternoon?"

"That's right, your honor."

Then she turned to the man on the opposite side of the room. "And the defense?"

"We still think she should have been charged, Judge. You have our request on file."

"Come on now," the first man interrupted. "You know there was no way you were going to pin this on her. When we picked them up, she had a broken collarbone, a black eye, and a left arm that was barely healed. She's a second victim, not a murderer, and you know it."

"Gentlemen," the Judge raised her voice slightly and nodded toward Audrey. "Can we agree that we are finished with this witness?"

Both men's voices sunk into a low murmur of agreement, and the Judge continued. "All right, let's plan to wrap this up this afternoon. Thank you for your help, Audrey. You and your parents may go."

Everyone stood, and Audrey looked up at the adults all around her, trying to read their expressions and figure out more clearly what was going on. Then she and her parents were led back out and down the hall to the main door. They walked around and looked at the fountain for a few minutes, then headed for the sidewalk. Audrey pulled at the neckline of her dress and tugged the back of it down as they walked toward the car.

She was surprised to hear her mother laugh suddenly, the tension from the courthouse falling away.

"You, my poor girl, are a wonder. We are so proud of you. I thought we should take you out for some kind of treat after all of this, but something tells me you'd just as soon go home and get that terrible dress off." Audrey hugged her mother tightly and nodded vigorously.

"You keep growing, girl, and you'll be as tall as me!" her father added. That sounded just fine to Audrey.

Present Day

Audrey looped the strap of her purse over one metal hook and slipped the hood of her rain jacket over the other before slamming the locker door shut and spinning the combination. She appreciated the space that the police department had given her in their often crowded locker room. The nylon jacket that they provided had ample pockets for her needs, and, with the heavy camera in tow, she appreciated being able to leave her purse behind. It had taken almost a full year working part-time as a police photographer for her to become accustomed to the routine, but now she felt like she had it down.

Audrey had finished college with a fine arts degree and had been working at building her own wedding photography business since then. It was a long slog, though, and in the meantime, she had taken on a variety of other jobs to help make ends meet. Once she found the job with the police department, her weeks had settled into an odd, erratic sort of rhythm rather than the nine-to-five that so many of her friends had adopted. Instead, she was frequently on-call for late-night police work, and on weekends she often spent both days photographing weddings and all of the events that had come to surround them. She felt confident that someday soon, her wedding photography business would take off, but for now, she needed both kinds of work to pay the bills.

Today she'd been called in the early morning hours before dawn to what looked to be some sort of mansion. The van pulled up a long, tree-lined drive and parked just beyond a tall set of steps. She waited her turn climbing out, giving the forensic team space to unload and organize their materials. Spring was just coming to the city, but she could already hear the birds and smell the lilacs that were beginning to bloom nearby. She knew almost nothing about the current case and allowed herself time to look carefully around her as they entered the building. Recessed ceiling lights in the foyer cast a slightly yellow hue over the sleek marble entryway. She followed the team into the front of the house, where a tall, elegantly curving staircase occupied center stage. Here, too, the medium was marble with an artful, black, wrought iron banister twisting its way up along the graceful curve. The body lay tangled at the bottom.

An older woman, 82, her notes said, lay sprawled in a loosely shaped 'S' with her head and arms near the lower step, her feet curving away toward the living room to their left. She wore a matching nightgown and robe, a peignoir set, Audrey'd heard them called, with thin, pink slippers that seemed designed to match. One of them lay apart from the body, the bottom of its thin sole still clean and white, unscuffed from any sort of wear. Audrey slipped paper booties over her shoes and got to work quickly, snapping photographs from every possible angle. She stepped thoughtfully around the scene, careful not to get in anyone's way as she focused in tightly on different aspects of the body, then backed the focus out to take in multiple views of the larger scene and confirm the scale of reference. She photographed the bottom step and then stood on it to get a different angle, but the stone was so slippery she had to grab the railing to catch her balance. Did anyone even use these stairs, she wondered, or were they just for show?

She finished gathering shots of the steps just above her and then moved carefully back down and over to where Detective Rodriguez was standing, watching the teamwork. "Anything else on this floor that you want me to get?" Audrey asked.

The detective lifted his chin in a quick acknowledgment and then led her around to the right, where an ornate elevator stood with its door halfway open. "Get some shots of this, would you? They're coming to finger-print this area next, and an engineer is coming in to look at what's going on with the door." Audrey worked systematically from the outside in and then back out. She started with the door and the track beneath it where a small stone appeared to be lodged in the groove. She took several shots of that before slipping inside. Unlike the entryway, this part of the house actually looked worn. The elevator's walls, originally a deep cream color, had faded spots scattered around at roughly shoulder height, as well as scuff marks lower down. The control panel indicated just three floors, the surface of each button worn in the center and on the right-hand edge. The bottom button stuck out at a slight angle. She focused her camera in closely on the panel capturing the details that her eyes had spotted.

"So what do you see, Scout?" Rodriguez stood next to the wall, his arms crossed in front of him as he watched her work. She emerged from the elevator finally and came to stand next to him. Audrey couldn't remember when he'd started calling her Scout, but she didn't mind. She knew that she had an eye for detail. It was one of the reasons why she'd been given the job.

"The bottom button on the panel doesn't look right to me."

Rodriguez studied her for a moment before dropping his arms and leaning in to look. He stepped back out. "Good call, I hadn't noticed that. Anything else?"

Audrey hung the camera back around her neck and gestured for the detective to follow her. She pointed to the staircase. "The steps are slippery. Either they weren't used much, or they were polished to look so nice they became dangerous." Rodriguez nodded in agreement, then stepped away as a young man in dark green coveralls knocked at the open door.

"Someone asked for an engineer?" The young man spoke, and as Rodriguez walked him back around to the elevator, Audrey continued to watch the team go about its painstaking work. This was officially an 'unattended death,' and she knew the question, in this case, was a simple one. Was it an accident or something more deliberate? Given the amount of money involved, she figured it probably would be a pretty important one to decipher.

More than an hour later, the team was finally wrapping up its work. The detectives had finished interviewing the cook, housekeeper, and gardener in the back of the house and come back out front to confer briefly. The body had been taken away, and Audrey took the last photographs that were needed at the top and bottom of the staircase. By the time they arrived back at the precinct, the sun was rising over the lowest of the buildings, and the smell of coffee was in the air. She thought it looked as though Detective Rodriguez might come and speak with her again, but his phone rang, so Audrey just waved and went on out. It was too late to go back to bed at that point, so she stopped into the coffee shop on the corner for a tall cup and a muffin to go. She was thankful that the light rain that had fallen earlier had quit. The walk back to her apartment didn't take long, and she enjoyed the spring sunshine on her shoulders as she walked. She waited until she'd unlocked the door, set everything down, and slipped off her jacket before taking the first sip. It was still blazing hot. She opened the lid, poured the steaming cup into a large red mug, and broke the muffin into several pieces on a small matching plate. Then she carried both over to her small dinette table where her laptop rested.

She'd gotten home late the night before and gone out early in the morning, so she shifted plugs, unhooking the laptop and reconnecting the charger for her hearing aids. She loved not having to constantly mess with batteries but making sure that they were fully charged for the day could be fiddly too. The ear infections that she fought as a child had continued into her teens, with the hearing loss growing a bit each time. She'd been prescribed her first hearing aids at fourteen and remembered being mortified the first day she had to go to school with them in. But there was no denying that they made a tremendous difference, and by college, she'd been in full militant mode with bright, neon pink ear molds that screamed defiance. Once she'd graduated, though, she'd opted for a more neutral tone and dumped more money than she had into a system with rechargeable batteries. Once it was ready to go, she lifted each aid out and placed them on the charger.

Quiet descended then, despite the open window. Audrey felt her shoulders relax a bit as she settled in front of her computer and ate her breakfast. She reviewed her calendar first, happy to see that the rest of her Thursday was clear. The wedding coming up would be her next priority, but first, she had work to do from the one she'd photographed the weekend before. That couple had very definite but sometimes opposing views on what they were looking for. She knew it would take her the first half of the day to sort through what she had and begin to make some decisions. The following day she was due in court. As a photographer, she wasn't called on to testify often. Still, this particular case relied so heavily on the physical evidence that the police had asked her to be available to answer any questions that might arise. She set an alert on her phone to be sure she was up in time.

As she finished the last bit of muffin, licking the tip of her finger to pick up the tiny crumbs, Audrey realized that she was up so early, she would have plenty of time to finish up her work and still have time for herself that afternoon. What should she do with her free time, she wondered? She thought about checking whether her mother was free for lunch or not, but with Mother's Day less than two days away, she decided not to. Her friend Katy was also gone, a nerve-wracking trip to meet her future in-laws that they had discussed ad nauseam for weeks. Audrey crossed her fingers briefly and hoped it was going well.

She sat back in her chair, sipping the last cold swallows of coffee. Perhaps she'd been too quick to dismiss Detective Rodriguez's offer to get breakfast together the other day. It had been less than three months since she and Charlie had broken things off or, dammit, since he'd walked off with that Cindy from his office. She shook her head, wondering why it still made her so mad, but, more importantly, why it had left her so reluctant to go out with anyone else. Audrey decided then and there that the next time Rodriguez asked, she would definitely say yes. In fact, she would look forward to it. Maybe she'd even muster the nerve to ask him. She closed the laptop and went to the sink, washing off her dishes and storing them in the cute wooden rack she'd bought the week before. She would take a nice long, hot shower and get to work. Then when she saw how much time she had left, she could figure out what to do with the rest of her day. Maybe she'd get her bike and camera and just go out and play.

8

Rod was standing in front of the mansion, waiting for the forensics van. He was glad to see that Scout was part of the team today and watched as she began working around the possible crime scene. He already had a feeling that this was going to be a complicated case to settle. The fact that a lot of money was involved meant that it might turn out to be pretty high profile and that never made anything easier. After he spoke with Audrey and then the engineer, he moved to the rear of the house, searching for his partner. He found Smitty sitting at a small, round table in what appeared to be a breakfast nook next to the much larger kitchen. Three individuals, he guessed them to be in their early to mid-fifties, were sitting with their backs ramrod straight and their eyes cast down. "What's up, Smitty? How's it going in here?"

"Good, Detective. This is Mr. and Mrs. Perez, the housekeeper and gardener, and Mrs. Garcia, the cook. Mrs. Garcia is the one who found the body."

Detective Rodriguez guessed from their names that their backgrounds might be similar to his own. "Hola, Señor, Señoras." The three looked up and met the detective's eyes at the sound of his Spanish. His parents had immigrated to the United States before he or his sister had been born, so he knew that his accent was pretty Americanized, but his vocabulary was solid. He looked to his partner to see what the situation was.

Smitty began, "Detective, all of them speak English, but I believe they might be more comfortable speaking with you in Spanish. I have assured them that we are not connected to immigration services, but they're leery just the same. They're also deeply saddened by the loss of

Mrs. Pelletier." Smitty nodded, stood, and offered his chair to his partner before turning back toward the front of the house. At the doorway, he paused, "Mrs. Perez is the housekeeper, so she is most familiar with things upstairs in Mrs. Pelletier's rooms."

Audrey rounded the corner just then, and Detective Rodriguez was happy to see her. "Audrey, would you please go up with Detective Smith and photograph the area on the third floor where Mrs. Pelletier's rooms are? Mrs. Perez, would you mind going with them, please?"

The woman was surprisingly tall. Her thick dark hair wound into a tidy bun with just a few stray pieces falling beside her ears. The detective noticed that she walked with an air that looked like a mixture of confidence and sorrow. Half an hour later, he had nearly finished his questioning when a young Hispanic man with the height and features of Mrs. Perez walked in accompanied by one of the uniformed officers. Detective Rodriguez stood as the young man introduced himself. "I'm Gabriel Perez. This is my father. I'd like to help if I might. I'm an attorney with the city." He looked to his father and asked, "¿Donde está mamá?"

Detective Rodriguez shook the young man's hand and pulled out an additional chair. "She's helping my partner to look at Mrs. Pelletier's rooms upstairs. Are you familiar with the house?"

The young man ignored the offered chair and stood next to his father instead. "Yes, I grew up here. May I go up to meet my mother? I'm worried she may be anxious, and she is not as confident in her English as she would like."

"Certainly, let's head up together. Do you two mind remaining here?"

They nodded their agreement, and the detective motioned one of the uniforms in to sit with them. Mrs. Garcia was offering him coffee as the detective led the young man upstairs. "Mr. Perez, I tried to assure them that we are not with immigration. Is that an issue here?"

"No, but in these times, it is a concern for all of us. My mother and father became citizens when I was a child, and Aunt Claudia is studying for the exam now." The young man hesitated then, and the detective waited for him to continue. He noted that Perez's shoulders sagged a bit as he continued. "The one they are concerned for is my uncle. He works as a long-haul trucker. I'm not sure where he is now, but they worry about him all the time."

"Your aunt says he's in Florida." The detective waved his hand in dismissal. "We don't care anything about that. Please assure them of that."

"Thank you, Detective. I will." He turned to greet his mother, who was standing in the hallway. "Thank you for calling me." He held his mother close and then stepped back. "Mama, I'm so sorry about Mrs. Pelletier."

"We all are, Son." She looked up at the detective and stepped to the side of the doorway. He looked into the room and saw Smitty watching as Audrey worked, photographing the room and its contents. She looked up to see the group in the doorway and pointed to the telephone beside the bed.

"Mrs. Pelletier had a landline with a base that lights up when a call comes in."

Smitty used his gloved hand to pick up the receiver.

"I wouldn't put that up to your . . ." Detective Rodriguez could hear the deafening dial tone from his place in the doorway.

"Ow, oh my God!" Smitty jumped, instantly pulling the receiver away.

"Ear. Sorry, Detective. I tried to warn you. The volume on it was probably set to the maximum."

"So I understand Mrs. Pelletier had been losing her hearing?" Rodriguez turned to Gabriel Perez, who nodded in agreement.

"Sí, yes, over the last ten years."

His mother pointed to the dressing table across the room as Smitty and Audrey walked over to it. "If you look in the top left drawer, you'll find her hearing aids."

Smitty pulled the drawer open, and they could see that the set was attached to a small charging station that included a cell phone.

"That's a beautiful set," Audrey spoke to the detective. "It's a high-end model." She continued into the bathroom and sitting room next door as she continued her work.

Detective Rodriguez turned to Mrs. Perez. "I take it from Mrs. Garcia that Mrs. Pelletier didn't usually come downstairs at night?"

"That's right. She always came up here after her dinner, about eight o'clock or so." Mrs. Perez pointed toward the armoire against the far wall in the sitting area. "Her television is in there, and there's a small refrigerator hidden inside as well. Either my sister-in-law or I usually saw her upstairs before we left for the night."

Detective Rodriguez looked around the room before turning back to speak with her. "Any idea what might have prompted her to come downstairs? Did you hear anything last night? Was anyone else here in the house?"

She shook her head. "No. We heard nothing. During the day, my husband and I were here bringing linens up and arranging the bedrooms for her children. They were expected tomorrow. The rooms are just down the hall here."

She gestured down the hallway past them, and the detective walked the length of it with her, looking in at the rooms, all of them beautiful but undisturbed. "Do you recall who was up here last, who saw Mrs. Pelletier last?"

"Sí, Claudia, and I were both here. We were with her checking that the rooms were how she wanted them. Mrs. Pelletier was a little tired, though, so Claudia brought her dinner upstairs to her, and we made sure she had everything she needed before we left."

"And when was that?"

Mrs. Perez looked at her son and then at the detective. There were tears in her eyes, and her voice caught on a sob, but she steadied herself and answered the question. "It was about 7:30. We saw her about 7:30 last night. Claudia and I went back downstairs and finished cleaning up the kitchen. Then we went over to our place. Claudia was expecting a call from her husband. He's on the road a lot. I didn't come back over this morning until she called to tell me she'd found Mrs. Pelletier." She dabbed at her eyes with a tissue and leaned just slightly on her son, who put a comforting arm around her.

"Is there anything else you need, Detective?" the son asked. "I think the three of them are all in a state of shock and would probably like to return to their cottage. Would that be all right?"

Detective Rodriguez looked at his partner, who lifted his chin slightly in agreement. "I think we're good, Gabriel, Mrs. Perez. We're sorry for your loss, and we appreciate your help." The group descended back down the stairs where Cesar Perez and Claudia Garcia were waiting. Detective

Rodriguez raised his hand to ask one more question. "What can you tell me about the elevator here? Do you all use it?"

Mr. Perez senior chose to answer, gesturing to his left as he did. "We usually take these back stairs, especially if we're working or cleaning, but yesterday, my wife and I used the elevator to bring all of the linens upstairs at once."

"And were you wearing boots or shoes with any sort of tread?"

He looked frightened and stared down at his boots. "I was wearing these. Is something wrong?"

"Can I see the bottom of them?" The man sat down and lifted one foot up and then the other. There was a pebble stuck in the tread of the left one, and the detective used the end of his pen to pry it out. The engineer had said that the issue with the elevator was the button, not the stone since the weight of the door could easily have dislodged it. Still, it was good to have that little question answered.

"Is there a problem?" The son asked, his voice leaden with concern, but Detective Rodriguez shook his head.

"No, it's fine. We just found a stone like this in the track of the elevator door." He looked over at the gardener. "Did you all use the elevator to come back down after you took the linens up?"

"No, no. We went back down the stairs."

"So you didn't know that it was stuck?"

The young man answered. "It got stuck a lot, Detective. As kids, we used to play tricks with it. One of the buttons would stick."

"She had been planning to replace it." Mrs. Garcia added. "Her late husband had it installed before he died. So it was getting old."

Both detectives shook their hands and watched as the sad threesome headed next door. The son lingered behind for a moment. He pulled out a pair of business cards from his pocket and handed one to each of them. "If you need any more information from them, I would appreciate it if you'd give me a call first. We all want to cooperate, but I need to know that they're being treated properly."

"Understood." Both detectives shook his hand, and Rodriguez pulled the door closed behind the young man as he left.

"Wonder what happens to all of them now that she's dead? Got to be a scary situation, don't you think?" Smitty asked as he pushed the chair back under the table.

Rodriguez nodded, "Definitely—add it to the list." It was their signal to move on. They stepped outside in time to see the tech van pull away. He and Smitty took half an hour more examining the grounds around the house, but there was little to see and nothing that stood out.

Friday morning came more quickly than Audrey wanted it to, but she was relieved that the stiffness in her legs was starting to let up. She'd had so much fun biking yesterday that she'd lost track of the time as well as the distance. Her first outing of the spring had left her sore and out of breath. Apparently, she needed to up her workout routine. In front of the courthouse, she looked around her at the dark stone blocks and the entryway that looked like a portcullis and thought that her first impressions as a child hadn't been that far off. More than a hundred and twenty-five years old, the amazing structure now had scaffolds and barricades where work was being done, but it still looked like something out of a Disney movie. Audrey wondered briefly what she'd looked like that first-time years ago, her dress too small, both hands holding tightly to her parents. It was hard to believe that twenty years had passed since then. Twenty years. She paused. Wait, hadn't Toby's dad been sentenced to twenty years? Why did she remember that number? Suddenly she could see his face so clearly as he passed by in the police car, his eyes fixed on hers.

She was glad to see a familiar face when she neared the courtroom. Detective Rodriguez stepped away from the wall where he'd been leaning, studying his phone, and welcomed her. "You ready for this, Scout?"

"Ready as I'll ever be," she shrugged. The benches that lined the halls now were a modern, metal style with a cool, brushed nickel finish that seemed out of place in the older building. "Hey Detective, are you able to look up when someone is going to be released from prison?"

"Sure, who you got in mind? Not an old boyfriend, I hope."

"No, no, someone from when I was little. His name's Gary Adams."

"Huh, why do I know that name?" He paused, his hand resting on the back of the nearest bench.

"He murdered his son Toby."

"Oh yeah," he leaned forward suddenly. "I remember my dad telling me about that case when I was thinking about becoming a cop. How do you know about it?" His eyes widened suddenly. "Wait, Markum, you're Audrey Markum. Oh, my God."

"Yup, that's me. As I was walking in, I was thinking back to my first visit here when I was taken in to talk to the judge. It's been twenty years."

"Is that all he got? For killing his kid? Jesus. I fuckin' hate this system sometimes."

She nodded, not sure exactly what to say after that outburst. She looked up at him. "So could you check for me?"

"Sure, sure, I can send a request right now. Just give me a second."

Within minutes they were led into the courtroom and the four-hour ordeal that too often measured out the tedium of police work. When they finished, she looked to see if the detective might invite her to lunch, but he was on his phone and then out the door with a couple of uniforms in his wake. It was starting to rain, so she caught the bus and walked the last block and a half home.

The whole morning she'd never been called on to say a thing. Her photographs had been sorted through and analyzed, displayed on the screen in front, and sometimes handed around the jury box as prints, but no one had a single question for her. In fact, the proceedings were so tedious that more than once, she'd sneaked a peek at her phone, but an odd sensation had swept over her then. How had it all come to be so routine to her, she wondered, the blood splatter, the murder scenes? Had she stopped recognizing the horror, the evil that she was photographing? How could that have happened?

Audrey still remembered the first crime scene she was called to. It was the middle of a hot, humid July night, down by the river. A three-quarter moon was hanging low in the sky, and the air was so still she could hear the small boat motor well before it came into view. They had been standing on a little-used dock, and the algae and other growth on the old wood filled the air with a fetid, organic scent that battled with the fresh smell of the tall weeds and the harsh notes of diesel fuel.

Normally a photographer wouldn't even have been called out at that point, but divers had been searching for the body for hours, the result of a miscommunication with a group of men who'd been fishing and drinking late into the night. English was not their first language, and it had taken time for an interpreter to be located and the men re-interviewed. Audrey had been called during the interim.

Once they had a better sense of what had happened, the divers found the body quickly. Audrey had her camera ready as the boat pulled up alongside the dock. They tossed the rope onto the deck, where one of the uniforms tied it up with an unhurried motion. Two officers reached over to help the divers in the boat, but it was still an awkward struggle to lift the man out and lay him on the dock. She'd felt sick at the sound the body made as it landed, slipping from their hands just above the wooden surface. It had been so hard to try and look professional while fighting to keep her hands from shaking. She'd had to hold her breath as she took the first series of shots. She still remembered the man's broad, empty-looking face, the sodden clothing, the single shoe, and the cell phone that had fallen out of his pocket as they dropped him those last few inches. The police hadn't cared about getting very many photos, so she'd worked quickly and then retreated to the van. She hadn't vomited, but it had been a near thing.

The following day there had been the smallest item in the paper about a man who'd died while swimming in the river. But she knew that wasn't right. He'd been wearing leather shoes, and his cell phone had been in his pocket. She'd felt sick again remembering what she'd seen and spent time looking through the paper for other jobs that morning, convinced that she would never be able to handle it all. But somehow, she had, and, as she walked the last block home, she wondered if that was a good thing or a bad thing in the end. It was definitely a weird way to make a living, she thought, as she sat down in front of her computer and entered the hours she'd spent into the electronic timesheet that she kept.

After a quick bite of lunch that she ate standing over the sink, she washed her hands and then settled down to continue reviewing the photographs from the last wedding. She knew that there were a number of them in the collection that both of them would love. It made a great contrast to the dirty footprints and sprays of blood that she'd spent her morning looking at.

When her phone rang at three-thirty, she was surprised to see how much time had gone by. She stood and stretched her back as she answered. "Hey Rodriguez, how's it going?"

"Good, good, pretty quiet for now. Listen, I was able to get that information you asked for. Any chance you'd like to catch a cup of coffee or dinner to talk it over?"

Here was the chance that Audrey had told herself to be ready for, but again, caution spoke first. "Sure, I'd like that. Can you meet for coffee in about 45 minutes? Syd's isn't far from the precinct."

"That sounds great. How about I meet you there at 4:30? I'll be off shift then."

"Sounds good, and thanks, Detective, for looking into it for me. I owe you one."

"Nah, nah, it was nothing. See you in a bit!" he responded cheerfully, and Audrey set her phone back down by the computer. There was enough time, she thought, for her to get a quick shower and maybe take a few extra minutes with her hair.

10

Rod pulled at the collar of his shirt and eased his tie apart just the slightest bit. God, he hated having to go to court. Give him an endless night shift or a mile-high stack of paperwork, anything but court. He was always worried that he'd say the wrong thing or get tripped up by an attorney's questions. At 34 years old, here he was, back in grade school, waiting in the wings for the winter play, worried that he was going to forget his lines or, worse, barf right then and there. He was staring at his phone, trying to settle his nerves, when he spotted the young photographer coming down the hallway. When she got closer, he called out.

"You ready for this, Scout?" He couldn't remember how long he'd been calling her that, since their first case together last summer, maybe. He'd heard it was only her second assignment. They were looking at a drug death over on the city's north side, the body sprawled across the stoop at the top of old, concrete steps. Audrey had been wrapping up her shots of the body as he and some uniforms were getting ready to fan out across the neighborhood.

"I'd check that way," she said, pointing off to their left.

"What makes you say that?"

"There's a bit of step crumbled here and the side of a footprint just there, at the edge of the sidewalk." Sure enough, she'd been right on the money, and they'd found the druggie's ex-wife tying off two streets down, sitting on the dead guy's bag of clothes. After that, he'd always just called her Scout and looked forward to seeing her whenever their paths happened to cross. He settled into the chair next to her in the courtroom and thought about what she'd asked him to look into.

Audrey Markum. He could still picture his dad saying that name to him, telling him about the fruitless time spent searching for the boy. He remembered, too, his dad's comment about what the child had seen. "I swear, Roddy, there wasn't but half an inch showing on the edge of that tennis shoe. I wish all detectives had eyes like that."

Rod had filed the conversation away after that until she'd mentioned the case that morning. He'd already sent the text requesting information on when Adams was to be released and hoped to hear back before they finished with their endless morning in court.

He'd heard nothing by the time they were done, though, and then got called out to another case before he'd had a chance to speak to her further. Back at his desk finally, he received a response and took a few minutes to look over the details of the case in the computer archives. Then he gave her a call. He was so glad she'd agreed to meet that he'd nearly missed the call from the vet reminding him to pick up Simple Simon on his way home.

The detective was only mildly alarmed by the cost of the vet bill, and he gave the dog a long nuzzle, figuring it was worth it if it meant he got a little more time with the pooch. He'd been named Simon initially but was dubbed Simple Simon after his third run-in with a skunk the first spring Rod'd had him. His mother had banned the dog from the house after that, and Rod had decided it was time they found a place of their own. He knew he should have moved out a few years earlier, but after his dad passed away, he'd worried about his mother and made excuses to stay. Simon had just forced his hand. They'd shared a studio apartment at first, the dog taking up nearly as much room as he did. Then his buddy had alerted him to the old house for sale just down the block from where he was staying. It needed work, a lot of work, it turned out, but it had been their home ever since, and Rod couldn't imagine being there without Simon. He hoped Scout, or rather, Audrey, liked dogs.

Since he'd first seen her, he'd been intrigued by her. His relationship with his partner Smitty's sister had grown stale, and by then, they'd both been looking for a graceful way to end it. But Smitty was a terrific part-ner, and Rod hadn't wanted it to affect their work together. One winter morning, though, when he'd said something about Leila's frustration with the dog, Smitty had begged him just to end it, that they were making themselves and everyone else around them miserable. It was a relief to have Smitty on board since it turned out to be exactly the right call.

Rod hadn't had a chance to work with Scout as often as he hoped since she was just part-time, but he'd enjoyed the time he'd spent around her, particularly on the case they'd been attending in court that morning. Her work had been excellent. He didn't think they would need her to clarify anything, but he'd liked having her there all the same. As they sat there, he watched her attention to the trial and wondered if she was as bored as he was. He saw her sneaking a peek at the email on her phone and figured he'd called it about right. He noticed, too, the hearing aids that she wore and wondered what the courtroom might sound like to her. He'd never met a young person with them before and was curious. She was very clear spoken, so he thought she probably wasn't deaf. Would it be rude to ask? He puzzled over that as the lawyers droned on and on.

God, she loved spring, Audrey thought as she walked to the coffee shop, sunlight streaming down through the trees with their bright, new leaves. Everyone on the sidewalk seemed a little more upbeat. People had their heads up and were looking around instead of hunkering down in their coats and scarves. The coffee shop even had a few tables set up outdoors, so after a quick check inside, she sat down to wait. Within minutes she spotted Rodriguez walking up the sidewalk, a big, gray-faced mutt ambling along at his side. She stood to meet them. "Who's this then?"

She bent over and rubbed the dog's head, scratching around his ears and back down under the white muzzle. The detective gestured Audrey into her seat and sat down as well, the dog dropping down comfortably at his feet.

"Sorry about that." He gestured with the leash. "This is Simon. He was at the vet for a check-up this afternoon, and I had to pick him up before they closed."

"How old?" She asked, reaching down to rub under his chin once more.

"Thirteen. I remember when he was a pup running around, getting into everything he could find. Hard to imagine it seeing him now. Do you have any pets?"

"No, not even goldfish, I'm afraid. I had allergies as a child, and that may have played a part in it."

"Does that relate to these?" He asked, tapping a finger against his ear.

"Partly, yeah. There were other issues but having allergies certainly didn't help." She thought about saying more but figured she'd wait to see if more questions arose first. She took a deep breath. "I'm anxious to hear what you learned."

"Oh, I'm so sorry, right. That's why we're here."

She smiled across at him. "Well, hopefully, that's not the only reason."

"Oh good," he breathed out. "I'm glad to hear that!" He stood and looped the leash over the back of his chair. "What can I get for you?"

Audrey quickly reviewed how many cups of coffee she'd already gone through that day and opted for tea instead. "Earl Gray with a little milk?"

"Coming up."

The dog took little notice of the unattended leash and instead dropped his chin down to rest on Audrey's foot. It was an endearing gesture, and she couldn't help but smile. When Rodriguez returned, the dog looked up for a second but then quickly settled back down.

"He seems to like me." Audrey took the cup of tea by the rim and set it down.

"Well, that makes two of us," Rodriguez answered and quickly busied himself tearing the bag open around two enormous chocolate chip cookies. "So, Gary Adams." He broke one of the cookies into several pieces before taking a section and leaning back in his chair. "You called it all right. He's not out yet, but his release is scheduled for Monday. The records indicated that there was no one specific to notify upon his release since his wife is listed as deceased."

"What happened to her? We heard that she went to live with her sister once the trial was over."

"Records indicated suicide just a couple of weeks ago."

"That is so sad."

"The address the prison had for her was at her sister's over in Lancaster, but there were no records of her having ever visited him."

"Well, that's not a surprise. Wasn't she hurt as well when the trial happened?"

"Yep, I was looking back over the case files this afternoon. The wife's medical records were a nightmare. She had a long history of broken bones, some internal injuries at one point, as well as fresh fractures at the time of the arrest."

"So she's lived relatively safely for twenty years and then kills herself? I wonder what triggered it after all this time?"

"I don't know. Maybe she was afraid of him getting out?"

"But you'd think that after all this time, she'd have had a better plan than that ready, especially if she was still afraid." Audrey paused, looking down the sidewalk as she considered the circumstances. "I wonder if she's really dead."

He looked up. "What makes you say that?"

"Well, she got away from him finally, and she's been living her life. Maybe she was afraid he'd come after her, and she figured this was the best way to keep herself safe."

Rod shrugged. "Well, it was just reported by her sister. I doubt if anyone looked into it. The police wouldn't care. I doubt the parole board would either."

Audrey leaned back in her chair. "You know, I hope she did fake it. I hope she's gotten this second chance and is making a new life for herself somewhere far away from Adams."

"Sounds good to me, but you look so sad. I'm sorry I brought it up."

Audrey took a sip of the tea and tipped a dollop of honey into it before stirring it once more. "No, I appreciate you looking into it for me."

"So, I gotta ask, is that case why you became a police photographer?"

"I'm not sure. I've always paid a lot of attention to details and the visual world around me." She lifted one shoulder. "It might have something to do with the hearing loss, too, I suppose. Mostly though, I just needed work. My main interest is wedding photography, but it's hard to get started in that business, and I needed a steady bit of income to carry me through."

"It's so gruesome, though, and you look so calm when you're doing it. That's not easy to pull off. I've seen plenty of rookies puking their guts out over scenes way less traumatic than the ones you've photographed. It can be pretty hard to handle."

Audrey worried for a few minutes about the implications of what he was saying. Did she seem cold-hearted or, worse, bloodthirsty in some way? "I don't know. It was hard at first. Maybe having the camera between me and the scene helps me to maintain my objectivity?" She laughed nervously. "I know that photographing weddings is a comforting counterbalance to have. How do you cope with it all?"

He reached for another bite of cookie and chewed thoughtfully for a minute. "My first partner was a real veteran, someone who'd been on the force for a long time but also in the Vietnam War before that. Nothing ever seemed to faze him, and so I worked pretty hard not to show what I was feeling. I wanted to handle things the way he did, I guess." He took a long sip of coffee. "So, do you think it matters about this guy getting out? Are you worried about it?"

"Not really, I suppose. Domestic violence was at its core, so I don't know that he'd be out looking for more victims. It's just . . ."

"What?"

He waited patiently while Audrey sipped again at her tea. "It feels silly even to mention it now. I mean, I was so little when it happened. I don't know why it would even matter. But I can remember sitting in the police car with my dad while a forensic team was in the woods going after the body, and this other cruiser drove past us, and I saw him. I don't know if he even saw me or knew that it was me who found Toby's body, but it felt like his eyes were boring right into me when he went by." She shivered briefly and set her cup back down. "See, even now, it still gives me the creeps. It's silly, I know."

He handed her a portion of the second cookie but held on to it for a half-second longer than needed as he looked at her. His voice was calm but firm. "There's nothing silly about any of that, trust me." He released the cookie then, and she smiled over at him.

"Thank you for that." She gestured around her. "For all of this. I'm going to let my mom and dad know what you told me when I'm home for Mother's Day this weekend."

"So, where's home?"

"West of the city, out in the townships. What about you?"

"Brookline, just above the river."

"Really? My dad still goes into Brookline to get his haircut. I used to ride along sometimes when I was little."

"My dad too. We might have seen each other growing up, fighting over a donut at the bakery, maybe."

"Well, we didn't get very far, did we?"

"Nope, I guess not. I traveled some with my family when I was young and again during college. I just didn't find any place that I liked better than here."

"Me either. I lived with a friend in Chicago for two years, but it wasn't for me. Pittsburgh is more my size, I guess. Well," she raised her cup. "We have more in common than we thought!" They pretended to clink the two paper cups together. "So, are you going home for a visit this weekend?"

"No, unfortunately, my dad passed away as I was finishing college, and my mom passed about a year ago. My sister invited me up to dinner with her wife and son, but I was thinking about working instead, maybe picking up a shift for someone who'd like to be home."

"That's nice of you. I'm sure they'll appreciate that." He shrugged and offered her the last piece of cookie before popping it in his mouth. The conversation was winding down, but Audrey was reluctant to let it end so quickly. "Any word on the rich lady with the elevator?"

"Hang on, just a sec." He stood and patted his pockets before going back inside the coffee shop. When he came back out, he was carrying two cups of water. He held the first one down in front of the dog, who lapped at it delicately until the cup was half gone, and then Rod poured in more from the second cup. When it seemed like the dog had had enough, he straightened back up and set the cups on the table. The dog lay back down then, his nose resettling onto Audrey's foot, this time creating a dark, wet ring. Rod leaned over, looking at her wet shoe. "Oops, sorry about that."

"It's nothing." She waved her hand to dismiss his concern.

"So, the rich lady, Mrs. Margot Pelletier, is quite the mystery. We're still working on that."

"Is there a lot of money involved? It looked like a pretty amazing house to me."

"Yep, you got it. She and her husband were both immigrants. She came over with her family between the wars, and her husband came on his own just after the Second World War. Apparently, he started with almost nothing and made his money in the steel industry."

"So, who's left now?"

"Well, that's part of what we're working on. They had three children." He ticked them off on his hand as he spoke. "One's been living in England, one in upstate New York, and the youngest, a daughter, out on the West Coast. They were all planning to be in town for Mother's Day. My partner's been checking out all of the financial angles, but we're just getting started. Nothing's come up so far. Who knows, maybe it was just a simple fall."

"I can't help but wonder what got her up out of bed in the night. Something made her take the time to put on a robe."

"Well, it was a windy night. Could it have been a branch or something that sounded like a knock on the door, maybe?"

"Does anyone know how bad her hearing was?"

"Pretty bad, apparently." He paused before proceeding with the speculation. "So you think it would have to have been something pretty loud?"

"Or maybe not a noise at all but something else."

"She still had a landline, so maybe a call?"

"I don't know, could be. Or the doorbell, if that has a light signal integrated into it like her phone. I didn't notice if she had one of those or not. They're not very expensive, though, and she clearly had money." Audrey shrugged and then raised her arms to stretch. "I think I've been sitting too long." The dog poked his head up at the sign of movement.

Detective Rodriguez gathered the cups and trash before going to pitch it in the bin near the door. When he returned, he picked up the leash and coaxed the dog out from his resting place under the table. "This was nice, Scout." Then, he paused, looking a little chagrined, "I mean, Audrey."

She laughed, "I don't think I've ever had a nickname before, except what my dad called me."

"And what's that?"

"DLR girl."

He tilted his head in confusion. "DLR?"

"Doesn't Look Right." Audrey laughed before continuing, "Apparently, it was a defining phrase from my youth. I used to say that lots of things didn't look right, especially food at first, and then lots of other things. When I started to complain about movies and TV shows, my folks got me a camera for my birthday. The card just said, '*make it look right.*' "She held up her hands in mock quotes.

"Kind of means the same thing as Scout, don't you think?"

"Scout's okay by me, a little less weird sounding, I think. Do your friends call you Stan or Stanley?"

"Oh, God, no," he bent over briefly as though in pain. "Stanley was what my mother used to call me when I was in trouble. Most of my friends just call me Rod. Listen, I'd like to talk to you some more about this case. Would you have some time tomorrow to maybe go back out to the house with me? I'd like to have another look around and get your take on things."

"Sure, I've got time. Should I bring my full gear?"

"Nah, no need for that. Would you like a ride?"

"That'd be great. I don't have a car here. I usually just ride out in the van with the team."

"Okay, then why don't I come for you around ten-thirty tomorrow, and when we're done, we can grab some lunch?"

"Sounds great." She waited while he typed her address into his phone, then gave the dog one last pat before heading back to her place. She thought maybe she was going to like the detective, Rod, she reminded herself. But she was relieved that she hadn't had to make a decision about dinner that night. She was glad, instead, for the plans to get together the next day.

CHAPTER

12

Audrey set an alarm and was up early. She put on her workout gear, thankful that she wouldn't need a heavy coat to get to her gym. She tossed her bag over her shoulder and peeled the wrapper off a granola bar as she walked. The sun was already up, and the flowering trees were turning her neighborhood into a spring wonderland. It was a beautiful day, and the six-block walk seemed to take no time at all. She signed in, switched into her workout shoes, and stowed her bag in a locker. As usual, the big screens scattered around the club were running different morning programs. She didn't like exercising with her hearing aids in, and the sets were difficult to hear given the general noise level, so she paid them little attention. She worked through her routine with the free weights before stepping onto the elliptical for a half-hour. She wasn't even halfway home before she'd emptied her tall water bottle.

She punched in the code on the grimy lock pad at the outer door and pushed through once she felt the click. It was kind of a sad-looking building, a large, older home that had been cut up into eight apartments. Its security system was an unsophisticated one that she imagined dozens of past tenants still knew the code to, but she figured it was better than nothing. She had a sturdy deadbolt on her own door and locked it religiously whenever she was home. After doing just that, she set the coffee to brew while she took a quick shower and washed her hair.

She kept her dark hair fairly short these days. It was easy to care for that way, and she hoped it never looked too awful if she was called out in the middle of the night. As she ate, Audrey turned to her email and confirmed a new lead on a wedding in June. Over on her website, she updated the calendar. She was eager to ask the couple from last weekend if they'd let her use the shot of them all laughing with the DJ for her gallery, but they were going to be honeymooning in Alaska until the end of the month, so she set a reminder in her phone to ask them later.

Audrey worked a while longer on the website before closing her laptop and getting ready. She brushed her teeth and added a touch of makeup before putting in her hearing aids and gathering her small camera and purse. The lovely morning was starting to cloud over, so she grabbed her bright red rain jacket and tossed it over her shoulder.

Rod was just pulling up to the curb as she stepped out of the apartment building. He leaned over to open her door, and she was a little disappointed not to see his dog in the car. "No pooch today?"

"Nah," he laughed. "He's home sleeping in a puddle of drool on my sofa."

She climbed in and hooked her seatbelt tight as he slowly pulled out into the line of traffic. Audrey loved how comfortable Rod was to talk to. They chatted easily about various topics, and she was quite surprised when they pulled into the long drive of the Pelletier home so soon. "Do they know we're coming?"

He nodded as they got out. The detective reached into the back seat and pulled out a worn Pirates jacket, checking the pocket for his badge. Audrey left her raincoat in the car but got the camera out to have it ready. "Yeah, I spoke with Mrs. Pelletier's older son this morning. He said the family would all be at the funeral home this morning making arrangements, but Mrs. Garcia, the cook, would be here to let us in. I spoke with Gabriel Perez this morning, too, but I assured him that we just wanted to look around again and wouldn't be questioning the staff. He seemed relieved that it wouldn't be necessary for him to come over."

The door opened quickly after Rod rang the bell. "Good morning, Detective Rodriguez." The sad-looking woman stepped aside to let them in, then closed the heavy door gently behind them. She was dressed modestly in a dark blue, loosely fitted dress. "I was told to expect you."

"Thank you, Mrs. Garcia. I just want my colleague, Ms. Markum, to take another look around with me."

"All right. I'll leave you to it then. My brother is out in the garden working if you need him, and his wife, my sister-in-law, is coming over this afternoon to take care of the cleaning. We were told that would be all right?" She twisted a tea towel in her hand as she walked them into the wide foyer. The detective spoke with the woman for a few minutes, but Audrey tuned it out, looking around her again at the broad staircase and the base of it where the body had lain. That area of the floor was polished to a high shine now, with no trace at all of the ugly scene from the week before. With a final nod, the woman departed for the back of the house while Audrey and the detective walked to the elevator. The door opened quickly at the touch of the call button.

"The engineer said the issue with the button was why the carriage wouldn't operate."

"I see. Were there fingerprints? Were they helpful?"

"No," he shook his head, "just the housekeeper's and her husband's. The panel was kept fairly clean. Apparently, smudges were a pet peeve of the owner, Mrs. Pelletier."

As they arrived at the third floor, Audrey stepped out onto the thick, light gray carpet that seemed to swallow every bit of sound. The air seemed stale, especially as they approached the older woman's bedroom. Audrey knew that the room had been searched and printed after she'd finished with her photographs the first time, but it was clear that it had been done with care and respect. Items on the tops of surfaces were left in a tidy line, and the bedclothes had been pulled up with pillows carefully placed. Audrey felt lost, not knowing what to look for. There were two tall windows with oak trees just beyond, their branches slower to leaf out than many others. Heavy drapes had been pulled open beside each window. The stale air probably meant that the temperatures outside hadn't warmed up enough yet to warrant opening them. "I remember these drapes were open when I got here last time. Had the police opened them?"

"No, actually, they were open when we arrived. We asked the staff and the children, and they all said that this high up, Mrs. Pelletier didn't feel like she needed them for privacy, and she liked having the light gradually brighten to wake her in the morning."

"Do we know anything about the robe? Did it typically lay on the bed or hang on a hook nearby?"

He laughed. "Apparently, along with smudges, the lady of the house couldn't abide hooks. She thought they were too lazy or something. Mrs. Garcia said that both the nightgown and robe hung on padded hangers in the closet."

"Wow, that's specific."

"Believe it or not, Mrs. Garcia told us she'd never seen Mrs. Pelletier downstairs in her nightclothes before. She always arrived for breakfast dressed and ready for her day."

"Does any staff sleep over, here in the house?"

He shook his head as he leaned against the bedroom doorway. "Nope, Mrs. Garcia's husband travels a lot for his work, so she shares the guest cottage with her brother and his wife." He checked his phone for the notes he'd made, then looked up at her again. "Husband's in Florida right now. He's a long-haul trucker up and down the east coast. Not expected back until early June, she said."

"I don't want to seem insulting, but wasn't she a little old to be living in such a big place all by herself?"

"We asked her kids that, and that was quite a sore point with them. But, aside from the hearing loss and needing glasses like most of us would at that age, she was perfectly healthy and resented it whenever her kids tried to bring up the subject. Her daughter says she kept asking her mother to move out to California with her, and the brother in New York wanted the same. I take it they were hoping to force the issue with her when they all got together for Mother's Day this weekend."

"I can see it from both sides, I guess. Too bad they didn't have a chance to sit down and work it out together."

Audrey walked from the windows along the side of the bed. She was surprised it was just a double, not a big king-sized one that her wealth might lead someone to expect. The coverlet, too, was very simple, a cotton quilt that looked as though it might have been homemade. The stitches were delicate, but with the slight unevenness, that hand working would have lent to them. On the bedside table were several paperback novels, the top one a recent thriller from a series that Audrey, too, had been enjoying. She found herself liking this woman and wishing that she could have met her.

In addition to the bed and nightstands, the room held a long, low chest of drawers on one side and a matching wooden vanity that was along the wall near the walk-in closet. Audrey sat down on the bench seat and was reminded of her mother's, although it paled in comparison. She hadn't had time to admire it when she was there before, but she did now. The piece was beautifully crafted in simple lines with a deep, polished wood surface. The marble top held a classic silver brush and mirror set that looked elegant but unused. Sure enough, when she opened the top right-hand drawer, there was a plain, plastic brush with black bristles intertwined with plenty of gray and white strands. "Everything had to look just right, didn't it, Mrs. Pelletier?" Audrey spoke softly, but Detective Rodriguez's eyebrows raised briefly in agreement. In the opposite drawer, Audrey could see where a hole had been cut in the back and an electrical cord brought in. The entire charging station was a much more elaborate set-up than her own, with a sleek cover that concealed the aids and a secondary station that held the phone. She guessed the phone was with the police now. Audrey lifted the lid and looked at the two pieces nestled snugly in the sculpted black foam. The light was green, indicating they were ready to go, but there was no one left to use them. She flicked the switch on the side to off. The set could be sold or donated, but there was no need to continue running electricity through them now. She looked up at Rod. "This is a nice set. You might ask if the family is interested in donating them. Aids are really expensive, and insurance doesn't usually help that much."

"I'll do that, thanks. That's a great idea."

Audrey walked the perimeter of the room again, pausing at each window, studying the depths of the large closet, stepping in, and looking around at the elaborate bathroom. Finally, she looked over at Detective Rodriguez, still standing in the doorway. "Nothing, absolutely nothing stands out to me. It just looks like a woman's bedroom with the things you'd expect to see and nothing that you wouldn't. It isn't particularly opulent or imposing, but everything is of fine quality and chosen with care." Audrey rested her hand on the foot of the bed, admiring again the colors and stitching of the coverlet.

"Well, Scout, I figure if *you* don't see anything amiss, then I don't think my partner or I missed anything either. It's just a puzzle." He shrugged and led her to the elevator down the hall from the bedroom. He pushed the button, and within just a few seconds, the carriage was there.

"It takes almost no time, doesn't it? At least when it's running, that is."

"Yep, now come with me over to the stairs and see what you think."

Audrey was struck again by the beauty of the staircase. It swept up one floor, made a graceful arc around one side of the central atria, then swept up again to the third floor. Tall windows circled the top of the space and filled the area with light. Given her nervousness with heights, Audrey took a firm grip of the railing as they began their descent. She paused and scuffed her foot across a step before looking up at the detective. "With shoes on, this feels all right, but you can tell they're a little slick. Those slippers she was wearing wouldn't have offered any skid resistance at all." Audrey paused again at the landing. "She made it this far, at least." They walked around the arc to the second section. "I imagine she would have held tightly to the banister, but perhaps when she turned to the next step, her hand slipped?"

"Or she was pushed. That's the question, isn't it?"

"How will we ever know?" Audrey asked as they reached the main floor. The detective shrugged.

"We may not. We're looking hard at the three children to see if there's anything going on with them that might have led one of them to hasten her death."

"And the staff?"

"It's possible that the gardener brought a stone or two inside with his boots. His wife says he was helping carry a lot of towels and bedclothes upstairs. They were preparing the rooms for the weekend, and a stone could easily have gotten trapped in the elevator opening. The door was stuck on it, but apparently, that wasn't the real issue. When they finished, they took the servants' stairs down, so they wouldn't have had any reason to call for or look at the elevator after that. It would have just descended on its own and then stuck." Rod waved his hand dismissively. "But really, we're not getting any kind of vibe from them at all. They seemed to like Mrs. Pelletier a lot, and now they're about to be homeless and out of work. They wouldn't have had any motive for harming her." The detective excused himself and went to tell Mrs. Garcia that they were leaving. She came and saw the door locked carefully behind them.

It was just starting to sprinkle, so they made a run for the car.

CHAPTER

13

Rod had enjoyed watching Scout examine the room in the big house. He and Smitty were grasping at straws to figure this one out. They were inclined to label it an accident and let everyone just get on with things, but the estate had turned out to be so large that there was too much at stake to make a snap judgment. He was relieved though, that Scout and her eagle eyes hadn't spotted anything that he and Smitty had missed.

They didn't get too wet dashing for the car in the driveway, but once he'd pulled over to the curb near the restaurant, the sky opened up, and torrential rain trapped them in the car. He took off his seatbelt and turned slightly to face Audrey right as she did the same thing. "The infamous spring showers." He pointed a finger in the air. "Were you planning to head out to your folks' place today?"

"What?" Audrey asked. Rod realized then how noisy the rain was, pounding on the roof of the car. He waved his hand. There wasn't anything that wouldn't keep until the storm let up. He grinned at her and mimed covering his ears with his hands.

"Pretty loud!" He spoke more firmly and clearly and was relieved to see her smile as well. After a few minutes more, the rain slowed, and they slipped on their jackets before emerging out onto the sidewalk. A few quick steps, and they were protected by the restaurant's wide awning. He'd picked his favorite sandwich shop. It was usually pretty busy, but the rain seemed to have thinned the crowd a bit. He held open the door and an older couple made their way out. After that, Audrey stepped in ahead of him, and they made their way to the counter to order.

"Have you been here before?"

Audrey barked out a quick laugh. "Are you kidding? They've been here forever. My dad used to bring me here when I was little, and my mom had to work."

"Not too touristy then?"

"No. What better idea could you have than to put French fries on top of a burger? But they're huge. I can't eat a whole one myself. Okay to split one?"

Glad he'd struck the right note, he followed her up to the counter and placed the order, adding a side of onion rings for good measure. The line snaked along toward the cash register until the trays were set in front of them, and he was able to pay. Audrey had spotted an empty table and made her way toward it, so he followed in her wake.

"This place is jumping today. I forgot how busy it gets on the weekend," Rod said as he set down his tray. Audrey draped her raincoat over the back of her chair and settled in across from him. He was pleased that here in the corner, the ambient noise was a little less.

"Mother's Day weekend may have brought some added crowds into the city too. Did you end up picking up a shift tomorrow?"

He nodded. "I did, traded for a day in June, so it's good. If I'm not called out, it'll give me more time to run down the information on the Pelletier family."

"May I?" Audrey reached for one of his onion rings, and he scooted the container into the center of the table. He loved how she looked after she took the first bite. "What a treat. I love these, and I never let myself eat them anymore. It sucks being an adult sometimes."

"My weakness is cereal. The sweeter, the better. Totally bad for you, I know, but I'm still a sucker for it. So, will there be a special menu for Mother's Day at your parents' house? Do you have a tradition around that?"

Audrey nodded before stealing one more onion ring, a small one that she popped in her mouth whole. She took a minute to swallow before answering. "My dad and I always used to fix breakfast for my mom. Nowadays, he makes bacon and eggs, and I bring the sticky buns. I've got some ordered for pick-up in the morning."

He hung his head for a second. "God, sticky buns, I love those. My sister-in-law makes great ones every Christmas."

She shrugged, "I'm not much of a baker, but I can shop. After breakfast, we'll probably go for a walk around the neighborhood if the weather's nice. It'll be great to catch up with them. I haven't been out there in more than a month. Spring is the start of wedding season."

"Would I have seen some of your pictures anywhere?"

"Not unless you've been looking for a wedding photographer."

He leaned back in his chair, raising his arms wide in mock fear. "Not me. A bunch of my friends from college all got married around the same time, but it's quieted down since then."

"I can show you my latest favorite." She paged through her phone to one of a bride and groom standing and waving on a sidewalk just as a spray of water was arcing through the air from a passing car. She turned it around for him to see.

"Oh no! I hope they were on their way out and not on their way in!"

"Luckily, they were. I hate that it happened, they were drenched, but I love the photograph." She flipped through her photos until she came to another favorite, this one of a forget-me-not with a tiny drop of water on one petal. She turned it for him to see. "When I take photos just for fun, I love to focus in, take close-ups. I sold some prints of this one."

"I like it. You do have an eye for details. How come you're not a detective?"

They began gathering up their trash. "Maybe because I'd rather take pictures of flowers than examine bodies, I guess."

"I certainly get that!" He took their trash and dropped it in the nearest bin before leading the way out. He held the door for her again and was delighted to see that the rain had ended. "Ah, perfect timing. Maybe the sun'll come out if we're lucky." Rod was disappointed that the ride back to her place took only a few minutes. He put the car in park and turned toward her. "This was great."

"What, even though I didn't see anything?" She teased. "I had a great time. I loved seeing the house again, especially without the dead body. Good luck sorting through all of it. I'll be anxious to hear more."

Rod took a breath and dared to push his luck a little bit further. "Would you like to have dinner with me on Tuesday or Wednesday? I'd love to hear about your weekend."

"Sure, Tuesday would be great. Would 7:00 be too late? I have a consultation with a couple, and they're not free until after five."

"7:00 sounds perfect. I'll see you then. Enjoy the time with your family!"

"I will!" She closed the door, and he watched as she made her way up the short flight of steps and into her building. Then he headed home to check in on Simon.

CHAPTER

14

Audrey was up extra early in the morning and stood at the curb by the bakery waiting for her ride. She knew that the fare would be high since it was a holiday, but it still beat the expense and aggravation of keeping a car in the city. After one particularly long winter of shoveling her car out of one snow-plowed bank after another, she'd given up on it altogether. Now, she lifted the bakery box to her nose and drank in the scent of the warm rolls. She spotted her driver then and was soon on her way. There was little traffic, given the holiday, and Audrey found herself enjoying the ride. The trees were coming into full bloom around the city, and flowers were sharing their bright colors from planters all over town.

On her way into the house, she paused to smell the lilac bushes that lined the driveway and threatened to take over the back porch. Her father opened the door, his hair longer than she remembered.

"They smell wonderful, don't they, Audie? I can't bear to trim them back, although I know I should. How are you doing?" He clasped her to him, and Audrey reached her arms around his neck and held tight. It had been too long since she'd been out there. His hair was much longer than usual, as well as a bit grayer than the last time she'd seen him. And perhaps he was a little thin? He led her in and then rushed over to the stove to tend to his pan of bacon. Her mother was at the table sipping her coffee and reading the news on her tablet.

"Hey, Mom. Happy Mother's Day!" Audrey leaned over and held her mother close. She stood back up and showed her the box. "I brought the good stuff."

"Wonderful, let's have a bite while we wait." Audrey set the box on the counter just as the coffee pot dinged, so she reached to pull down another coffee mug. She refilled her dad's cup, set it down near him on the counter, then poured a mug for herself and set it and the newly filled carafe on the table across from her mom.

"So what's with the hair, Dad?" Audrey asked, looking from one parent to the other. She took one of the sticky buns, cut it into several pieces, and set them on a small plate. She offered her dad a bite before setting the plate on the table.

"Hmmm, just as good as I remember." Her mother hummed with pleasure.

"What're you saying, DLR girl? You don't like the look?" Her dad grabbed her around the waist in a quick squeeze."

Audrey giggled, "*Doesn't look right* is exactly right. What gives?"

Her mother waved her hand in the air and said. "He's protesting something or other, but he's not saying what. I'm hoping it's just a phase he's going through. Maybe male menopause or something?" Her father responded by leaning over her mother's shoulder and blowing a loud raspberry just behind her ear. Laughter filled the kitchen, and Audrey leaned back in her chair, delighted to be home. She sipped at her coffee and soaked in the scene around her. She was so lucky, she thought, to have this house and these people to come home to. She wondered why she didn't do it more often.

"So, what's new around here?" she asked.

"Not too much," her mother answered. "I still like my work, but I've started exploring some other opportunities too."

"I'm surprised."

"Nursing just isn't what it was, I'm afraid. It's all about computers and data collection and less and less time spent working with patients. I'm ready for something new."

"What about you, Dad? Are you thinking about changing careers too?"

He collected the bacon on a plate and set it to warm in the toaster oven while he scrambled the eggs. "No, now that I'm finally the boss, I'm never quitting. How's your work going?"

"It's good. The last couple I photographed was a little crabby, but I can't complain. Plus, I got to take pictures in the most beautiful mansion."

"A society wedding?" Her mother asked as she sampled another bite.

"No, unfortunately." Audrey shook her head, "although you could certainly hold a beautiful one there." She could easily imagine a young bride gliding down the elegant staircase and hoped that perhaps that image would begin to push away the one of the woman's body sprawled at the base. "Did you read in the paper about a wealthy woman dying? Her name was Pelletier."

Her father collected the bacon and eggs and brought them to the table. "I think I did see something about that." Audrey didn't want to ruin the lovely breakfast with police talk, so she steered the conversation into safer territory. "So what's happening in the neighborhood, Mom?"

The breakfast was as delicious as Audrey remembered, the bacon smoky and crisp, the eggs soft and cheesy. The sticky buns were the perfect accompaniment, and the three of them were soon stuffed to the gills. Her father pushed his chair back as he began gathering up the empty plates.

"That was wonderful, but it's a good thing we don't eat like that all the time." Her mother spoke as she folded her napkin and settled it on the table. "I'd be as big as a house. Why don't we go for a walk? Mitch, that can wait can't it?"

"Sure. Let me just put some water in the pan before I grab my jacket."

Audrey and her mother stood in the driveway, enjoying the lilacs while they waited for her father to join them. A few neighbors were out on their porches or working in their flower gardens as they walked past. Audrey noted a lot of new faces but also some familiar ones. As they approached Sandy's house, she skipped ahead and rang the bell. Sandy's husband, Oscar, came to the door and engulfed her in a warm hug before Sandy waddled forward to get a hug of her own. She was eight months pregnant with twins, and it showed. "How are you doing?" Audrey squeezed her friend's hands.

"We're fine, tired of waiting and terrified of what comes next, but other than that . . ."

Audrey laughed. "I get that, but I also know you're going to be awesome parents. How's your mom doing?" Sandy and her husband had moved in to save some money towards a house of their own, but her mother's health had taken a turn for the worse, so they'd decided to stay awhile longer.

"Better, I think. We're spoiling her this morning for Mother's Day. Want to come in?" Sandy held the door wide.

"No, no, that's okay. I just wanted to check and see how you're doing. I can't wait to meet the little ones." They made plans to get together sometime soon, and Audrey returned to her parents. She knew that they hoped for grandchildren, too, but Audrey did her best to avoid conversations about men and dating, especially since the fiasco with Charlie. Seeing Detective Rodriguez was exciting, but for now, she decided to keep it to herself. It did remind her, though, of the news she'd heard. "Mom, Dad, did you know that Mr. Adams is getting out of jail soon, tomorrow actually?"

Her mother stopped. "How can that be? After what he did?"

"It's been twenty years now, but I wanted to ask you, what did you hear about Toby's mother after all of that happened?"

Her father answered. "I'm not sure, but it wasn't long after he went to prison that their house was sold."

"Wasn't there talk of her going to a sister's, somewhere in the center of the state?" Her mother asked.

"That's what I thought, but I couldn't remember who said it," Audrey answered. "When I found out about his release, the detective told me that Mrs. Adams committed suicide just within the last few weeks. She'd been living with her sister."

"That is so sad, after all she went through. It seems so long ago. I wonder why it happened now?" Audrey's mother looked over at her dad.

"Maybe she was afraid of him getting out? I don't know."

"That's what I wondered," Audrey added. "I was also wondering whether it was true or not."

"Well, if it were me, I'd have headed for the hills and not come back. What a despicable man he was." Audrey's mother commented.

Audrey nodded in agreement and turned to her father. "He scared me. Dad, did you say their house was sold? I'm hoping he won't have any reason to return to the neighborhood."

"I can't imagine why he would," her father added as they resumed their walk.

Audrey squared her shoulders and took her mother's arm. "Okay, no more of that. It's Mother's Day, and we're busy celebrating, not worrying about the past. Should we check if there are any good old movies on TV this afternoon?"

"Oh, your dad recorded *To Have and Have Not* when it was on the other night. Let's watch that."

By nine-thirty, Audrey was home and settling down in front of her computer. It had been a wonderful visit, but now it was time to gear up for wedding season. She thought about putting on some background music but decided she was just too tired to listen anymore, so she got to work in the quiet.

By noon it had proven to be a pretty slow Mother's Day in the city. Detective Rodriguez had gone out with a team at nine, but the circumstances hadn't required much. A family argument had led to a heart attack. It was unfortunate, but the man had been in ill health for quite some time, so there was no need to open an investigation. Rod grabbed a coffee and pastry on his way back to the station and settled back down at his computer.

Smitty was home with his wife and her family, but he had spent the day before with Mrs. Pelletier's accountant. Rod read through his notes carefully and found that the estate was considerable. It included two ongoing businesses, one domestic and the other a large multinational one, the tremendous house with all of its grounds and staff, in addition to over five million dollars in other assets. There was little or no debt.

Although the accountant had not seen the will recently, it was his understanding that everything would be divided equitably among the Pelletier children. He reported that Mrs. Pelletier had included the staff in her plans as well. The house was to remain unsold as long as the present staff wanted to work and live there. After that, it was left to the heirs to decide. All three children stood to receive enormous payouts. Smitty's notes on the accountant himself were straightforward as well. The family had employed his father's firm for decades. The young man had met the woman's children on several occasions but didn't seem to have formed any real impressions of them. He noted, however, that Mrs. Pelletier was quite bright and had a keen understanding of both the businesses and the family assets. In fact, they had recently met for their quarterly review of her accounts and to discuss the coming year.

Rod shifted in his chair, suddenly aware of the time that was passing. He had to find more information. The funeral was to be held on Wednesday, provided the medical examiner released the body before then. So far, though, the office had not reached a conclusion. The cause of death had been determined, a broken neck and a severed spinal column due to the fall, while the time was estimated between three and four in the morning. The toxicology report indicated no alcohol or drugs in her system other than a mild analgesic, probably for arthritis. The question was whether or not the circumstances warranted more of an examination. The number of overdose deaths in the city had skyrocketed in recent years, and the medical examiner's office was understandably swamped. As the department's liaison to the lab, Rod felt inclined to ease everyone's burden by pushing for a death-by-accident decision. Still, with an estate this large, there was just no way that anyone was comfortable with a rush to judgment. Every 'I' needed to be dotted, every 'T' crossed. Why was she out of bed? And how did she end up at the bottom of the stairs? Those two questions remained unanswered.

The detective stood and stretched as high as his arms would go, then leaned forward until his hands lay flat on the floor in front of him. His back was starting to ache from the crappy chair, and he was no further along than he'd been when he started. First thing that morning, he had requested phone and financial records for the house and all three of Mrs. Pelletier's children, as well as those for the cook, her husband, her brother, the gardener, and his wife, the housekeeper. With the holiday, every office he tapped seemed to be working with a skeleton staff, though, and the minutes were ticking by.

There were three Pelletier children. The oldest, Arnaud Pelletier, Jr., lived on the outskirts of London. Or he had. It was reported that he had entered the US in the last week, two days before his mother's death. In his preliminary interview, Rod had discovered that the man, now in his mid-fifties, was newly divorced. His ex-wife was British, and they had no children. The man had mentioned that he was considering living in the big house as he worked to get back on his feet in America. He said that he had planned to speak with his mother about it that weekend. When Rod asked about his finances, Pelletier had blanched and swallowed hard before answering. "Bad, I have to admit, they're really bad. The business my wife and I had together was going well. I persuaded her into expanding our holdings, but then political events in England took a turn." Rod remembered him leaning over in his chair and running his hands through his hair before sitting back up. "The business was in her name, or her family's, rather, but the money we borrowed was all in mine. They pulled together and survived financially, but I didn't." He had been fiddling nervously with something from his pocket when what looked like an AA coin fell to the floor. He picked it up, seemingly without embarrassment, and was turning it slowly. Rod recognized the red color. It belonged to someone whose sobriety was still relatively new. "I lost my way, Detective, and I'm trying to fight my way back."

"So you needed your mother's money right now, didn't you?" He'd asked, putting an edge into the question.

"No!" The son stood abruptly, then turned his head away. Rod waited the few minutes that it took him to pull himself together. Finally, the man turned around and looked at the detective directly. "I needed my mother a lot more than I needed her money."

Rod had found his story convincing, but he watched carefully as the financial records finally began to load. Arnaud Pelletier, Jr., hadn't exaggerated when he said they were bad. A cursory look found him nearly two million dollars in debt. And, it didn't look as though the entire sum had been borrowed at once the way he'd described. The man had been doing a lot of borrowing for quite some time, and Rod wondered if there were other addictions besides alcohol that might have been draining his funds. The first of the phone records arrived as Rod read through the financials, so he switched screens. It appeared that Arnaud, Jr. had two cell phones, one for use in England and one for the US. On the US line, there were several calls to a law firm specializing in bankruptcy here in Pittsburgh, one call in the last month to his mother's house and one the week before to his sister in California.

Rodriguez decided to call the son and get a feel for how he was sounding that day and to verify where he had been staying before the death, as well as after. He dialed the number for the US cell, but it rang without being answered. An automated voice asked him to leave a message. He wondered briefly if he had just been busy or if Pelletier had looked at the Caller ID and deliberately not answered. Either option was pissing him off. "Mr. Pelletier, this is homicide Detective Rodriguez. Please call this number as soon as you can to schedule a follow-up interview regarding your mother's death." Rod said no more than that, hoping it might spark just enough panic to persuade the man to cooperate.

Rod noticed the hour, then, as well as the frustrating fact that the rest of the records he'd requested had still not arrived. The change of shift was coming in, so he briefed his replacement and headed home. He figured Simon would appreciate the reasonably early night. Rod looked forward to a walk around the neighborhood with him so that he could enjoy the last bit of sunshine. It seemed as though it might be the last dry day for some time. Bad luck all the way around, he decided.

When the call came at four o'clock Monday morning, Audrey was in no mood to respond. She'd enjoyed the day with her parents but hadn't gotten home until after nine. After which, she had worked for a bit and then taken hours to fall asleep. Nights where her brain churned and churned, were so frustrating, and then to be awakened so early on top of that was awful. She lay back on her pillow and considered calling in sick, passing on the assignment, but that didn't seem right. No one wanted to get up at that hour. It wasn't just her.

She dressed in the short time it took for a car to arrive and was at the precinct by four-thirty. It was raining again, of course. She gathered her gear and the rain jacket from her locker before heading out to the van. It was the same group she'd gone out with to the Pelletier house, so there was a lot of chatter among them. It wasn't entirely clear to Audrey what they were saying in the noisy van, but she got a sense that they were hoping for another spotless mansion to examine. Unfortunately, the scene was entirely different, a tiny, dark, filthy parking lot in one of the city's rougher areas. There had been a late-night shooting behind a dance club. There were two people dead, as well as several more injured, and the press had beaten the police to the scene. She figured someone's social media post must have alerted them. Several uniforms set up blockades and tape to keep the curious out, but it was slow going, and the team waited in the van for several minutes before they could get through. Finally, they were waved into the area, and Detective Rodriguez met them, opening the door and briefing them on what was needed. Audrey made a point of standing next to him so that she could be sure to hear what he was saying over the rain and other noise.

Once the group was unloaded and pulling their gear from the back, the detective turned to Audrey. With rain running off his ball cap and down the back of his jacket, he bent close to ask, "How was your Mother's Day?"

"It was great. It feels like it was about ten minutes ago, but other than that . . ."

"I know what you mean!"

She pulled her hood up and straightened the wide bill to provide as much cover as she could. The rain wouldn't affect the camera, but she had to be able to see well to take the quality of photographs and references that would be needed. The noise of the pounding rain made further conversation impossible, so she smiled at the detective and got to work.

They were there for hours. Dawn came with increasing light, but no more than a brief let up to the rain. Tarps and lights had been set up, but the scene remained an incredible mess. Audrey didn't know how anyone could distinguish the blood from the rain and mud. She had worked as usual, in fits and starts, waiting and watching for direction as the team moved around the scene. The media had been there through the early morning and their cameras and flashes added to the difficulty she was already experiencing with the rain.

When they finally arrived back at the precinct, she sat down on the wooden bench in the locker room and watched as puddles formed beneath her. She was exhausted and peeled off the rain gear slowly, glad that she had thought to bring a spare set of clothes. She took a quick, warm shower and dressed, then packed up the rest of her gear and headed out. She was surprised to see Detective Rodriguez, unoccupied, standing near the door. "Hey, there," she called.

He stood and moved toward her. "Hey, yourself. Terrible way to start the day, don't you think?"

"The worst. Are you still on duty?"

"I told the captain I was going to take a little time and get breakfast before I wade back into everything. Do you have some time? Want to join me?"

"I would." She paused. "I'm beat, aren't you?"

"I'm trying not to think about it. Don't name it, don't claim it. Isn't that what they say?" The rain had finally quit for good, and it looked as though it might turn into a nice day after all. The clouds were thinning, and it seemed to be warming a bit. They took their time walking the few blocks to a diner. They passed a local newsstand, one of the few left in the city now that the Post-Gazette had stopped its print edition. In its place, the display was filled with glossy magazines and the rash of tabloids that had come to fill the void. Audrey was almost past it when one of them caught her eye. The headline screamed **DEADLY MOTHER'S DAY SHOOTING** and showed a full-page photograph from the night's crime scene. What was disturbing was the clear image of herself standing to the side with her camera in her hand. Audrey remembered the moment when the rain had let up for just a second, and she'd thrown her hood back to get a broader look at the scene. She stopped and stared. "Oh, my God, I look horrible!"

"No, you don't. Are you kidding? You look like an intrepid reporter or something. Fresh-faced but fearless, you know?"

"Oh, please, I look like a drowned rat is what I look like." She fingered her damp bangs, trying to fluff them out a little bit. "I think I need a haircut."

"Well, come on and get some breakfast. No need to worry about these rags anyway. They'll be garbage by the afternoon."

"I hope you're right," She echoed, and they turned again toward breakfast and a pot of hot coffee.

CHAPTER

17

Gary Adams emerged into the morning rain twenty years older and forty-five pounds heavier than when he'd gone in. The slight edge he had possessed before he went in had been whittled and honed until he was an angry, powerful man with no one and nowhere to direct his rage. He'd been signing for his belongings when the desk clerk offered her condolences on the death of his wife. He pretended to accept her kindness, but inside it burned. The dumb bitch. She spends twenty years waiting for him, and then boom, she kills herself? Just before he's supposed to get out? What was she thinking? That cunt of a sister that she was living with probably had something to do with it, he figured. Well fuck, he didn't need her, not really. With no family, no place to go, nothing to do, he decided he was truly free, and as he stepped through the open doorway, he smiled.

He caught a bus, transferred twice, and found himself in the heart of the city. He had just $750 in his pocket and no clear idea what to do first, but the sun was starting to come out, and he welcomed the light. He thought he'd pick up a couple of newspapers and maybe start looking for work. He also bought some cheap coffee and a sandwich from the shop, then brushed off the water before sitting down on an old wooden bench in a small park. There was a basketball court and playground nearby, but both were deserted. He folded the wrapper down around the sandwich and then took a look at the gaudy cover of the first tabloid. There'd been a shooting the night before. It was in a part of town he'd never been to, and he wondered what sort of lowlifes had been taken out. He'd met all types where he'd been and had respect for no one. Whoever they were, they probably deserved it, he thought. His eyes shifted focus finally from the plastic draped bodies to the others at the scene. That one girl looked familiar somehow. He sat looking at the photograph for a long time until the image finally clicked. It was that little bitch that had discovered Toby's body. He knew he would remember that face.

God damn it. He crushed the paper in rage. He had had everything under control. For weeks he'd gone through his grieving father routine, and then the steam had gone out of everyone's interest, and it had been allowed to drop. For almost a month, he'd been able to go about his business in peace, no more of that whiny little puke of a son. Even the wife had finally quit bawling when he was around. Everything was looking good until that nosey little neighbor girl had ruined everything. *Audrey Markum.* He straightened the page out and finally located the name on the caption, confirming his suspicions. So she worked for the police department now. Wasn't that convenient? Damn, he was probably the one who'd gotten her started on her career. He was due something for that, for all of it, for that matter. He ate the last bite of the sandwich and made a decision. He needed to find this bitch and make sure she understood just what she had cost him.

18

Audrey was clearly flagging by the time they finished their meal, so Rod waited with her for the bus and then returned to work. He picked up a copy of the tabloid on his way back to the station and pulled it out to look at the photo again. He didn't think she'd looked awful at all. He liked how she looked, in person and in the picture. He thought the photograph made her look a little younger, maybe. As he tucked the paper away in his bag, he thought for a few minutes about their plan for dinner the next night and considered restaurant options. He pictured them walking along the waterfront, if the rain would ever end, and figured that Jerome's might split the difference between fancy and run of the mill. Once he'd made a reservation, he put his mind back on the task ahead of him.

Arnaud Pelletier, Jr. had finally responded to his call and was due in the station house any minute. It was time to nail down a timeline of the man's actions before his mother's death. Rod looked up as a uniformed officer led Pelletier back to his desk. At least he was prompt. Rod gave him that. He stood. "Mr. Pelletier, thank you for coming in again." They shook hands, and the detective indicated the seat next to his desk.

"Arnaud, please, just Arnaud." Rod noticed that the man was neatly dressed, not flashy but regular. He wore jeans and a flannel shirt that looked new. His hair was a dark brown with a few gray flecks, grown a little long and shaggy over the ears.

"Arnaud, then. As you know, we haven't been able to close out this investigation yet, and I have just a few more questions for you. I want to go back over your timeline here in the city. When exactly did you get in?"

Arnaud reached in his back pocket and pulled out his passport. It was slightly curled from being in his pocket, and the cover was a bit worn. He opened it to a back page where a faint visa stamp was located. "You can see here where it was stamped. I got in Wednesday at seven PM." Unfortunately, although you could read the time, the date was not legible at all. Detective Rodriguez copied down the passport number before returning it to him. He would have to make a call once they finished.

"And where did you go once you arrived?"

Arnaud tucked the passport back into his pocket and settled back into the chair. "Well, it felt like it took forever to get through customs, but I guess I was out of there by eight o'clock, eight-thirty, maybe? My sister had arranged an Airbnb for us starting on Thursday, so I was planning to get a hotel for the night."

"You didn't go straight to your mother's? The staff was preparing rooms for all of you."

"I know." He nodded, "but the three of us wanted to get together first before we saw Mom so that we'd all be on the same page." Arnaud showed him the address of the rental apartment on his phone, and the detective made note of it.

"So, which hotel did you stay in?"

"Well, here's the thing. I've been having a rough time lately, as I said. I got in a cab at the airport, and I was planning to go to a hotel, but then I panicked a bit, so I asked the cabbie to drive me to a meeting instead. It was at some random church downtown. I don't think it ended until about ten."

"So then you went to a hotel?"

"Well, no, by then, I was hungry, so I got a bite to eat at a diner near the church. After that, I was still wide-awake, and it seemed stupid to waste money on a hotel room. There was a movie theater a couple of blocks over, and I caught a late show. The diner was still open when the movie let out, so I went back there afterward."

"What time was that?"

He shrugged. "Not sure, maybe three AM or thereabouts? After I finished eating, I walked around for a little while. Then I fell asleep on a bench outside the library building. It wasn't that cold out, and I figured I'd use the library's Wi-Fi once it opened."

The detective leaned back in his chair and looked at the man, allowing the silence to draw out before he spoke. "We've identified the time of your mother's death at around four o'clock that morning." Rod spread his hands out wide. "You know this looks bad, right? You have a key and ready access to the house. Can you think of anyone in all of that meandering who could identify you, confirm your whereabouts that night? Maybe start with the meeting?"

Arnaud leaned over in his chair, resting his elbows on his knees and running his hands through his hair again. He looked up finally, his face ashen and drawn looking. "You do know that the second 'A' stands for anonymous, right?"

"The theater then? The diner, maybe? What kind of receipts have you got?"

Arnaud rubbed his hands back and forth across the tops of his legs and closed his eyes. Then he let his arms drop to his sides and looked directly into the detective's eyes. "Look, I've got nothing. My credit card's maxed out, so I paid cash all night. I couldn't even tell you the name of the god-damned diner or the church. The movie was an old one, whatever that *Heaven Can Wait* was a remake of. Maybe you can find the theater's name that way, but I don't imagine there's a soul who could identify me as being there. I can tell you I was one of very few in the audience who wasn't sleeping, having sex, or dealing drugs." He ticked the items off on his fingers. "Maybe that'd make me stand out, but I wouldn't want to bet on it."

"So tell me this. What do you think happened to your mother that night, the stairs, the fall? Did you call the house when you got in? What do you think got her out of bed at that hour?"

"I have no idea, Detective, and I've been thinking about nothing else since it happened. I didn't call. I was going to see her in just a couple of days."

"What do you know about the elevator?"

"Nothing, just that it's old. I never use it when I'm there. My dad had it installed for my mom before he died. That's been over fifteen years now."

The detective closed the folder and set down the pad he was writing on. "All right. I'm going to look into the theater angle and see if I can find anyone to verify that you were there. Are you staying at your mother's home now?"

Pelletier stood, stuffing his hands into his pockets. "No, I'm at the Airbnb for now. We're planning on going over to the house together after the service. But right now, I need to find a meeting because, Goddammit, I want a drink."

The detective walked him to the front of the station and then returned to his desk. He ran a quick search for theaters that were open late, but the first pass, at least, turned up nothing. There were just no easy answers in this case. He thought—time to bring in the daughter and the other son.

Audrey was relieved to get home and shuck off her shoes and the rest of the dirt and grime that she'd picked up from the morning's crime scene. She felt energized after breakfast but still gave herself an hour or so of downtime before getting back to work. She brewed a small pot of coffee and spent several hours collecting and editing photographs before getting up and slipping into a spring dress with a short, lightweight, matching jacket. It was one of her go-to wedding outfits, and just putting it on seemed to lift her mood. She packed up her two gear bags, double-checked the battery supplies, and tucked a small folding umbrella into one outside pocket and a bottle of water into the other. Her phone lit up, indicating that the driver had arrived, so she hustled downstairs and into the welcoming sunshine.

The morning's downpour had made way for a beautifully sunny afternoon. Audrey sat back and enjoyed the ride that took her to the outer edge of the borough, where the two grooms had rented a semi-rustic venue for the event. She had done a wedding there in the fall and remembered a large, open barn area where the dinner and dancing would probably happen and a loft above the western end where the ceremony and cocktails usually took place. The wedding was scheduled for five o'clock with drinks, dinner, and dancing to follow. The plan was to take the posed, family, and wedding party photographs ahead of the service rather than after. She was thrilled that the rain had stopped and hoped the grass had dried enough for them to walk out away from the structure a bit.

Audrey had met Jeff and Jerry through friends from her old neighborhood and was pleased to see how relaxed and at ease they looked as she stepped out of the car. "You two look great!" She beamed at the two grooms, both splendid looking in matching black tuxes with deep red and purple vests. She hugged them each carefully so that no one's outfit would be harmed.

"Come on in and meet our families and friends." Jeff led her into the front of the barn. A small combo was setting up their musical equipment in the corner, and a festive group was standing in bunches of three and four, taking turns at the large mirror that stood just down the short hallway near the restrooms. Jeff led her around and introduced her to his family, and then Jerry took over and did the same. Audrey had wondered if there would be any tension in the air as the two men wed, but she happily saw no indications of it in the lively group.

"Okay, everyone, should we get some photographs going? I think the light is at the perfect angle right now for us to get some good shots." She looked at the group and asked, "Who has the list for me?"

A young woman in her late teens came forward with a small black portfolio and handed it to Audrey. "Hi, I'm Jeff's sister, Caitlyn. He asked me to be your helper."

Audrey took the portfolio from her and opened it to a neat list of formal and informal shots that they were hoping she would capture. "This is terrific, Caitlyn, and I'd love to have an assistant today. Let me set my bags over here, and you can start organizing the first group. We'll start with the larger ones and then work our way down to the two grooms so that everyone else can go on in and enjoy some cocktails. How's that sound?" She asked the question to the room as a whole and saw heads nodding in agreement as Caitlyn began gathering up the first set.

The sunshine coming through the trees had the rich, buttery warmth of late afternoon, and Audrey was confident that the formal photographs were going to look fantastic. They were a friendly, happy group for one thing, and there seemed to be no bickering whatsoever, a welcome change from a recent wedding she'd done where a groomsman and bridesmaid had ended their own engagement plans just before the ceremony. The tears and pauses for make-up repairs had been endless.

Today's group finally dispersed inside while she took the last few photographs of the two men. She saw them teasing each other and straightening each other's ties between poses as she switched one lens for another. Audrey quickly snapped a few candid shots of the moment and thought that they might turn out to be the best of the day. They stood then and posed for a few more before Audrey was satisfied, and Caitlyn declared their formal list complete.

Jeff and Jerry led the way into the barn, where their mothers had begun organizing the guests into seats for the ceremony. The loft area had been decorated simply but beautifully with baskets of spring flowers that included tulips in more shades than Audrey could count. She took a few shots of the decor and then took a seat at the back. She quietly swapped out batteries and lenses as the ceremony proceeded, then stood to catch the happy shots of the two men walking together back down the center aisle. She stepped to the side, and the two of them hugged and kissed family and friends as an informal receiving line developed to the left of the bar area. Two young waitresses were circulating platters of hors d'oeuvres, and Audrey moved carefully around the scene, snapping candid shots.

Once dinner was announced, the guests trooped down the stairs to the main dining area and shuffled around searching out name cards. Audrey took a few moments to confer with Caitlyn so that she had a good sense of which groups were at each table. Then the two new husbands were introduced and the room filled with applause and laughter as they danced their way down the stairs and into the room. Dinner was served buffet-style, and Audrey took a seat near the back with her camera and bags well out of everyone's way. Once the line thinned, she fixed herself a small plate and ate a few quick mouthfuls before getting back to work.

By the time the car let her out at her place later that evening, Audrey felt exhausted but satisfied. It had been an incredibly long and tiring day beginning with the crime scene and carrying forward through the lovely reception. She was anxious to take a look at what she'd captured but even more anxious to get out of the painful dress shoes she was wearing. On the sidewalk, she paused to enter a tip for the driver on her phone. A shadow darted to her left, and she looked up quickly but saw nothing. "Just a branch," she said to try and reassure herself, but she rapidly punched in the buttons for the outside lock and then yanked open the heavy outer door. She slammed it closed behind her and moved quickly to let herself into her place and lock the deadbolt.

Once she was safely inside, her shoulders relaxed immediately. She set down her bags in the entryway, toed off her shoes, and moved toward the kitchen, where she put the kettle on to make a cup of tea and grabbed a yogurt out of the refrigerator. She checked that the charger was plugged in correctly and then removed her aids for the night. The quiet that descended was blissful. She couldn't get through her day or her work without the aids, but they simply could not filter sounds the way ears could. The endless cacophony from a day like today was exhausting. She shrugged off her jacket and settled it on the back of one of her bar stools before pouring the water for tea and locating one of her protein bars to round out her snack. She synced up the camera and computer and began eating as the photographs loaded. She'd taken hundreds of shots, so she put her feet up and waited. It was too late to do much more than that for tonight, but there were just a couple of shots that she wanted to take a quick look at. She paged through them until she came to the couple she'd caught between poses before the service. In the first, Jeff's face was turned away a bit, but the second shot was great. The two men practically vibrated with love and excitement, and the photograph had captured it perfectly. She was thrilled.

Audrey continued flipping through them, looking for the one with their mothers that she hoped was also going to be terrific. She had come upon the two women late in the evening. Their shoes were off, and Jeff's mother had pulled off her earrings and laid them on the table. They were having a good-natured conversation about surrogacy versus adoption when their sons appeared. The looks on the two men's faces were priceless when Jerry's mother said, "What, just 'cause you're gay doesn't mean we're not expecting grandchildren! Come on!" All of them had dissolved into laughter, and Audrey had done her best to capture the foursome. There, there it was, and it was excellent if she did say so herself. They looked just right, she thought and closed the computer for the night.

As soon as Arnaud was on his way out the door, Rod was in communication with the Airbnb owner from the address that he'd been given. Although they were not comfortable telling him any of the details of the rental, they did indicate that the same party had rented it Wednesday night through Friday. Since Arnaud had stated that the reservation didn't begin until Thursday night, Rod's next call was to the sister. Renee Pelletier was at the rental when Rod called, but the day was growing late, so he agreed to meet her there in the morning. That gave him time to delve into what else he could find on both her and the brothers electronically.

He began with the daughter, and although there was little on her outside of a few social media sites, her husband's name was Harold Crane, and he appeared often in the public record. He was a city councilman for a small town in California that had suffered considerable damage in the fires of a year ago. The town had lost its hospital as well as a number of school buildings, and the recovery seemed to be slow going. With so many cities in need, most of them much better known, the city council had been struggling to meet their town's needs and suffering in the press for their efforts. Rod wondered, not for the first time, why anyone would want to go into politics. He also wondered what the wife's role in all of that controversy would be, especially with a middle school-aged daughter to care for. That had to be tough.

He read further and decided that this seemed to be the single, most unlucky family he had run into in a long time. The second son, Jules Pelletier, appeared to have considerable troubles of his own, as his name was easily spotted in the press too. He was listed as a younger partner in a dental practice that had been dragged into a scandal. The Buffalo news carried ongoing reports about the senior member's arrest on charges that he had been abusing female patients for years. The practice had gone into receivership as the trial dragged into a second month. The detective wondered where that left Jules. It didn't appear as though he'd been implicated in any way, but it certainly wasn't a situation that would inspire confidence in would-be patients.

Rod's partner Smitty had been drafted to work with the larger team that was following up on the dance club murders, so Rod was left on his own to tie up loose ends regarding the older woman's death. The body had been released for burial, and his chief had told him in no uncertain terms that it was time to fish or cut bait on the investigation. Accident or murder, it was time to reach a decision. Unfortunately for the detective, the more he learned about the woman's children, the murkier the case became. Everyone in the family seemed to be in dire straits and in need of the inheritance money.

Rod planned to head to the rental first thing in the morning, but shortly after he arrived, he'd been called to a death about a mile from the precinct house. Word from the station was that just after he got his call, a body had been spotted in one of the dumpsters in an alley behind several restaurants. He was thrilled that he'd caught the earlier callout and wasn't available to go dumpster diving, especially since he'd put on one of his nicer shirts and ties for his date that night with Audrey.

It was closer to noon by the time he got everything settled enough to go and interview Renee Pelletier. When he called, she mentioned that both of her brothers were out, so he felt the timing might work to his advantage after all. The rental unit turned out to be an older home on the south side of the city. He knocked on the door and waited, wondering what sort of reception he would get. When the woman opened the door, grief-stricken seemed to be the best description he had for her. In her late forties, Renee Pelletier appeared to be trim and fit, but there was a sag to her shoulders that made her look older than her years. Her hair was light brown and straight, cut to curve along the bottom of her jawline, but now it was a mess, as though she'd been dragging her hands through it repeatedly. "Detective Rodriguez, please come in."

The detective stepped inside and held his badge out for her to see. She glanced at it briefly, and he stowed it back in his pocket. "I'm sorry to be so much later than I had planned, Ms. Pelletier. Or do you go by Mrs.?"

"It's Mrs. Crane, Renee Crane, but it doesn't matter. Nothing matters as far as I can tell."

"I'm sorry for your loss, Mrs. Crane." He waited by the door.

"Come in, please. I've just made another pot of coffee. Would you like some?"

"That would be fine, thank you." The house had looked rather old from the outside, but the interior had been renovated in an oddly modern style and was filled with sleek wood surfaces and miles of chrome. The living room was slightly sunken and held a large sectional sofa opposite a massive TV screen. The fabric was patterned in navy blue and lent the space a darkened air in spite of the bright fixtures. She re-entered the room carrying a bamboo tray with coffee cups, a tall, slim carafe, and a bowl of sugar.

"I'm sorry, I can't seem to find any milk or cream to go with it." She settled onto a portion of the sofa perpendicular to where he was sitting.

"Black is fine, thank you." He waited while she poured the two cups and then set his on the table in front of him while he pulled out the small notepad he liked to use. "Mrs. Crane, I spoke with your brother, Arnaud, yesterday about the timeline for his visit here in the city. Can you begin by explaining your whereabouts to me, beginning with the time of your arrival?"

She held the mug in her hands but didn't drink as her eyes shifted to the ceiling and then returned to his face. "I lied to my brothers, Detective."

"Lied how?"

She breathed out a deep sigh and set the untouched cup on the coffee table near his. "I told them that this rental started on Thursday afternoon. We were planning to sit down together that evening to talk about our mother and make some plans for taking care of her. Jules and Arnaud were both going to stay here that night, and then we were to meet our mother on Friday morning for brunch. We had planned to spend

Mother's Day weekend with her, all of us together. That hadn't happened since we were children."

"So, the lie?" He waited and watched as emotions seemed to move across her face in waves, guilt, despair, anger, disappointment.

"I rented this place beginning on Wednesday, Detective. I was being selfish, wanting it to myself for just one evening. One evening to myself was all I wanted."

"Why is that?"

"This has been the most difficult year of my life. I thought I deserved just a tiny bit of quiet. You read about the fires in California last year, right?"

He nodded. "It must have been difficult for you."

"Difficult doesn't begin to describe it, let me tell you. Fleeing with my daughter in the car, driving through those walls of fire, not knowing where my husband was, if he was alive or if my daughter and I would live to reach safety?" Tears filled her eyes, and she reached for the box of tissues on the table. She pulled two out, leaving the box in her lap. "My daughter and I were at one shelter, and then we were moved to a second one as the fire advanced. It was three days before we saw my husband or even knew that he had survived. My best friend and her two sons did not. Everything happened so fast, and with so much confusion, it's impossible to describe to someone who hasn't been through it."

"And your husband and daughter, are they well now?"

She blew her nose and dabbed at her eyes before setting the tissue box beside her on the sofa and reaching for her cup. She took a long drink, and Rod waited as she assembled her answer. "Physically, we're all well. We were lucky. We had no injuries from the fire, only exhaustion and fear. But the emotional turmoil didn't end when the fires were extinguished. My husband is a city councilman for Redmund, or what's left of it. We lost our only hospital and several schools in the town, including my daughter's middle school. He's spent the last year begging and arguing with the state and utility companies, trying to find money that just isn't there. Everywhere had damage, and there isn't enough money to go around. My daughter's class has been meeting at one building after another with a revolving door of teachers who can't or won't stay because of the fires. She's a wreck. We all are. A few weeks ago, I talked with my mom about what was going on, and she invited Hilly and me to stay with her this summer. She was already looking into tutors for me so that we could help Hilly catch up. I hadn't told my brothers any of that. I just figured I'd bring it up when we had our dinner together. But that never happened." She leaned back and held her arm against her forehead before raking her fingers through her hair again.

Rod hated to put an edge to his question but felt that he had to, given the circumstances. "So you're telling me you were here the night that your mother died. Is there anyone who can corroborate that? Did you speak to anyone, maybe order food or have anything else delivered here?"

"No, I didn't. I wish I had, but I wasn't feeling well once I got here. I stopped at a market on my way in from the airport and picked up a few things for dinner and breakfast in the morning. We were going to have our big meal delivered, so there wasn't much else that we needed."

"Did you make any calls, contact your husband or daughter maybe?"

She shook her head and sat without speaking for several minutes. He allowed the silence to grow, hoping that the discomfort might force her to say more. But rather than saying anything else, she seemed to collapse in on herself. Finally, she brought her gaze up to meet his. "No, I told you I was being selfish. I texted my family when the plane touched down, but I turned my phone off after that. I wanted to be alone, and now . . ." She reached for the tissue box again, pulled one out, and dabbed at her eyes before crushing it in her hand.

"What can you tell me about your mother's habits? I'm curious what you think she was doing on the stairs."

"I imagine the elevator was stuck again. She told me she'd had someone in to work on it recently, but they said there wasn't much they could do aside from replacing the entire control panel. Given the age of the thing, I don't imagine my mother thought it was worth it. I'm pretty sure she intended to replace and upgrade the whole thing."

"And her staff? Do you have any thoughts about them?"

She leaned back against the sofa, the crumpled tissue resting in her lap. "They've always seemed like nice people to me. We've known them forever. Of course, we never see much of Mr. Garcia because he's on the road, but the others we know well."

"Did your mother have any difficulty communicating with them?" Her expression changed but seemed to stop just short of rolling her eyes at him.

"Detective, my mother spoke four languages and was busy learning a fifth one when she died. I'm certain they had no difficulty communicating at all." Rodriguez folded his notepad shut and stood up. There was little more that he thought he'd get from the woman today.

"Can you tell me where I can find your brother Jules, Mrs. Crane?"

She finished dabbing at her nose and stood, gathering up the tissues and tossing them into a wastebasket nearby. "He was meeting a colleague from dental school for lunch." She tilted her head. "You know he was struggling with his practice, right?"

"Yes, I had read that. When do you expect him back?"

"I don't know. The owners were kind enough to extend our rental here through the end of the week. Do you know if we're going to be allowed to have the service tomorrow?"

"Yes, the body's been released. I'm going to call Jules and arrange to talk with him. If you speak with him first, please have him call me." He handed her his card and let himself out the door. As he swapped his notepad for keys to the car, he marveled again at the misfortune that this family was experiencing. Now, dammit, he had two people unaccounted for at the time of the mother's death. Please let Jules be a blabbermouth. He begged, a social media hound with fifty witnesses to his whereabouts.

By the time Audrey got home the next day, she was exhausted. For the second morning in a row, she'd been called out to a crime scene. This time, a dumpster held the body of a teenaged boy. The detective in charge, Myra Angellini, was a woman in her mid-thirties. She was not someone that Audrey had worked with before, but she had an excellent reputation within the department's crew of technicians. She and a pair of uniforms had secured the scene looking for clues to the boy's identity as well as possible reasons for his demise. Audrey had resisted as long as she could, but finally, she'd had no choice but to climb inside the dumpster to get the shots that she needed. She photographed the body first. His face was spotted with acne, his T-shirt torn and filthy. Both of his arms were covered in scabs, and she wondered if he was even fifteen yet. After that, the technicians carefully lifted the body out, and she began photographing what had been under him. A tech started lifting out the items, which included two bags of garbage from a nearby restaurant. It looked as though they had been shoved to one end of the dumpster, and Audrey noted that the one closer to the body had been torn open at the top. A takeout container had been pulled out and opened, and Audrey thought about how often she'd ask for a container to take leftovers home and then forget it on the table. This one held two pieces of fried chicken and probably would have been a prized find for the boy. However, it looked as though he'd taken only a few bites of it.

Audrey pointed it out to the tech working next to her. "I think he crawled in to eat, don't you?" The man nodded and gestured for one of the uniforms to step closer so that he could share their thinking.

Audrey took the rest of her photographs as the tech talked further with his partner. They examined the body a little more before bagging it up for transport.

"So, what do you think killed him?" Audrey heard the detective ask, but the man shrugged and moved to follow the body.

"I won't know until the autopsy. He's covered in sores and needle marks, but the marks aren't that fresh. There are no obvious signs of trauma, but he's skinny as hell, so maybe he was sick or starving. I got no idea." The two of them moved away as the body was lifted into the van. A third tech stepped up to take their place and continued removing items from the dumpster. Audrey had climbed up onto the top edge and was sitting there, continuing to take photographs, when she spotted something metal beneath where the boy had been lying.

"There, what's that?" She pointed, and the tech used tongs to withdraw a set of dog tags. They were surprisingly clean, Audrey thought. She looked over as he was dropping them into a small plastic bag. "Maybe they were in his pocket?" she mused aloud, and the tech handed her the bag. She took it by the top edge and swung her legs over the side, jumping down just as Detective Angellini strode up.

"What have you got there?" The detective reached out and took the baggie from her but didn't move any closer. Audrey knew she smelled pretty rank and didn't blame Angellini for keeping her distance. "Anything else?" The detective directed the question to both Audrey and the remaining technician. The man shook his head and tossed the last few items out of the bin before climbing out himself.

"No," he gestured at Audrey. "She spotted the dog tags, but I didn't see anything else of interest."

"Except the takeout container," Audrey added and looked up at the detective. "There was a container of fried chicken pulled out of the restaurant's garbage, and it looked like it had a few bites out of it." Detective Angellini lowered her head for a moment, and Audrey thought she heard her say "poor kid" very quietly before raising her head and addressing the tech and another uniform.

"Let's wrap things up here, folks. We'll leave this one for the coroner unless anyone found someone who says they saw something." The group began cleaning up the site, and Audrey stood leaning against the van, waiting. The detective walked over to her but stopped again before getting too close.

Audrey held up her hand and spoke first. "I know. I smell like a dumpster. Don't get too close."

"There's nothing like the glamour of police work, is there? Nice job spotting the dog tags. I'd offer you a ride back . . ."

She tilted her head, but the sentence dropped off, and Audrey held her hand up again. "I get it. I'm happy to ride back with the other stinky technicians." They were finished packing up by then, and Audrey waved goodbye as she stepped into the van.

Once she got home, Audrey knew she'd never do any quality work feeling the way she did, so she took a long, hot shower, washed every bit of grime out of her hair, and pulled on some comfortable paint-splattered sweats. Her five o'clock appointment had called to say they needed to reschedule so she made herself a cup of tea and took it to the couch to read. She was relieved that Rod had understood when she asked to postpone their dinner plans until the following night.

"Oh no, so you ended up with the dumpster duty? And I was counting my blessings that I'd managed to miss it. I'm sorry. Was it as bad as I imagine?"

"Worse. The garbage and everything was nasty, but mostly, it was really sad. He was only a boy, probably a young runaway who was just looking for something to eat. I don't see how you do it, Detective."

"I'm sorry, Audrey. I know that must have been bad. Listen, get some rest and spend some quality time with your wedding photographs and we'll get together tomorrow. In fact, would you be interested in going to the Pelletier funeral with me first? Once it's over, we could go and have some dinner." Given the good impressions she had of the woman, Audrey hesitated only briefly, and they'd settled their plans quickly.

Now with the cup of tea only half gone, she settled deeper into the cushions and was out. It was after five before she woke up and sat rubbing the sleep from her eyes. She finished the now cold drink and went looking in her refrigerator for some dinner. Darn it. She didn't even have any eggs. She'd meant to go shopping, but thinking she would be going out that night, she'd put it off. She considered ordering some carryout, but that wasn't going to answer the question of what she'd eat for breakfast or lunch the next day.

She set the empty cup in the sink and went back to her bedroom to put on some real clothes. It wasn't far to the market, but she didn't want to go out looking like some pathetic cat lady or something. She put her hearing aids back in, emptied her backpack except for her wallet, and then added an extra grocery bag in case she bought more than she was planning on. That seemed to happen all the time. She pulled on a lightweight hoodie and shouldered the pack. Once she got outside, Audrey realized what a beautiful day she had been missing. Once again, the morning's rain had given way to bright sunshine and a nearly cloudless sky. She had to watch for puddles on the sidewalk, but it felt terrific to be out on such a wonderful evening. She was glad she had opted against having something delivered.

The market was a small one, family-owned with old-fashioned bins of fresh fruits and vegetables flanking the door. Audrey picked a basket off the stack and added some fruit and avocados before ducking inside. The air was filled with the enticing scent of freshly roasted chicken, so she selected one from the warming shelf. She picked a small container of salad to go with it and then headed to the back of the store for milk and eggs. A fresh loaf of bread, and she was ready to go. The line was short, and she recognized the man behind the checkout. "Hey, Sunan, how're you doing?"

"Good, Miss Audrey, real good. Did you have a nice Mothers' Day?"

"Yep, and you?" He looked over his shoulder where his mother-in-law often stood. She was a beautiful older woman who regularly wore saris in blazing reds and blues with intricate patterns Audrey found fascinating. Still, the woman was also more than a little frightening. Her frequently dour demeanor always seemed so at odds with her beauty.

Today she was nowhere around, so he turned back to Audrey with a pleased look on his face. "It was very nice. My sisters-in-law took Mama out to lunch, so my wife and I were able to spend the day with our son and his family."

"That's great. How's the new baby doing?" Audrey could see the joy in his face before he even spoke. He helped her sort things into the backpack and bag and then held it while she ran her card.

"She's beautiful, just beautiful, all of that dark hair!" His black hair was cut in a tight buzz, but he gestured to imitate the baby's thick mop.

"That's wonderful. I'll look forward to seeing her in here sometime."

"I think I'll have her this Thursday morning for a bit, so stop in then."

"Will do!"

Audrey took her time walking back, stopping to chat with a couple walking their dog and then pausing for a few minutes to sit with a fellow tenant on the steps of their building. Decades ago, the grand house had been converted into several apartments, but the front porch was still much like its neighbors, a broad wooden landing flanked by a stone wall and steps. She hated to go inside, but her neighbor had left in a cab, and it was growing darker out. Hunger was getting the best of her when she noticed that the overhead light outside seemed to have burned out recently. She was a little uneasy in the darkened entryway as she fumbled, punching the code in the lock. Once inside, she set her groceries down and locked her door behind her. She sent a quick email to the landlord about the light before unpacking the food and fixing herself some dinner.

When she finished, Audrey took her plate and cup to the sink and set them down, then paused a moment to look out her kitchen window. Some movement had caught her eye, and she stared hard at the sidewalk where it looked as though a man had stepped behind a pear tree that was just coming into bloom. She could have sworn he was looking right at her, but the wind caught a branch full of blossoms, and, as they swayed, he disappeared. Audrey closed the blinds and then rechecked the locks on her front door before heading into the bedroom.

CHAPTER

22

Early Wednesday morning, Gary Adams was awakened by a baby's screams from the apartment next door. He turned over and tried to stuff the thin, worthless pillow against his ear, but the sound still penetrated. After fifteen endless minutes, the crying finally subsided, and he was drifting back to sleep. Then a garbage truck began lumbering down the alley behind his unit, and the neighbor upstairs turned on a morning television program. Goddamn place, it was as noisy as prison. He'd felt lucky when he found the small apartment on Monday afternoon, but now he was already regretting the choice. Luckily, a former inmate had steered him toward a bar not far away from where he'd easily been hired as a bouncer, paid under the table, of course. He figured he'd stick out the week in this hellhole, and then, once he got paid, he'd look for something a step up. He needed to find a real job, but first, he was going to deal with that little bitch whose picture had been in the paper.

The day before, he'd discovered that the computer access at the library wasn't bad. The speed was fast, and there didn't appear to be much oversight of the patrons' internet usage. Unless someone was caught watching porn, little notice was taken. He'd always been good with computers, but his time inside had allowed him to develop some additional, off-market skills. In less than a half-hour, he had located her residence within about a three-block radius. He'd found a gym nearby where she appeared to be a member. It also looked as though there was a small grocery store within the same area. He thought either one would be an easy spot to watch for her. There were two coffee shops within the area, as well, so he decided to start his search there.

Later that night, as he lay in bed, he took a moment to delight in the success he'd had with his strategy. Hers was not an easy neighborhood to watch. There were a few larger apartment buildings on her block and a few coffee shops and other businesses in the area, but like so much of the city, it was mostly filled with blocks of single-family homes. He almost wished he had a dog to walk so that he'd have a chance of blending in. As he was getting ready to head to the bar to work, he'd spotted her walking to the market. Once she left the apartment, he took a moment to reach up and unscrew the front light before following her. He'd seen her talking nonstop with the shop's apparent owner and then walking home. Alone. He lingered outside as long as he could, delighting in her apparent unease at the dark entryway. He watched the front of the building until he could see her in the window. Once he was sure she'd spotted him, he took off, pleased with himself at how quickly he'd figured her out.

Now in the light of day, the question was what to do about her. He knew that eventually, he'd have to kill her so that he could get on with other things in his life. But first, he wanted to get under her skin, to put real fear into her. He wanted her looking over her shoulder every second. Then he'd kill her. Since he was already awake, he decided to get started by picking up a few groceries at her local market. He figured he'd get the owner talking, probably get a lot more information to use in his scare-the-shit-out-of-her project. She looked like such a goody-two-shoes. He'd bet she was an early riser too.

23

Audrey rolled over in bed and couldn't believe it when she saw the time. Nine-thirty, when was the last time she'd slept in that late? Plus, even better, she hadn't started her day before dawn staring into death. She spread out flat on her back and stretched all of her limbs before getting up and slipping on her favorite, faded gray hoodie. She thought for a moment about the beautiful gown and robe that Mrs. Pelletier had been wearing, but that was never going to be her. Now, maybe if she had a sexy, overnight date, but that didn't seem to be in the immediate future, although she was looking forward to dinner with Rod that evening. She paused, looking at herself in the mirror, her hair flattened on one side, the hoodie spotted and stained. Yeah, she was a catch for sure. Coffee, what she needed was coffee, then she could figure everything else out.

Two cups later, she was feeling human and ready to face the day. She pitied her nine-to-five, Monday through Friday, always-working-overtime friends, knowing how lucky she was not to be caught up in that grind. She ran wet hands through her hair and then slipped into yoga pants and a lightweight top. Her gym bag didn't need much, so she dropped in a protein bar, then washed and refilled the water bottle. It looked as though their recent pattern of morning rain and afternoon sun was holding. She stepped out into the morning's wet aftermath wishing she'd taken the time to bring her camera. She loved how the city looked, with drops of rain still clinging to everything. By the time she finished her workout, everything would have dried off and returned to its normal, grimy state. What the hell? She'd only gone about a block and her day was pretty free. Why not go back for it?

Within a few minutes, she was back on the sidewalk, camera in hand, lost in the look of her neighborhood. It was one of the older ones in the city, and although it wasn't wholly gentrified yet, it did have some buildings that had been beautifully restored with their intricate brickwork and tiny city gardens. Audrey took her time focusing in on little details, like a clump of wet dandelions leaning against a fireplug. Then she expanded her focus to capture the set of businesses that were lined up across the street. The coffee shop had its outside tables wiped dry and back in use with the old-fashioned, laminated menus tucked between the salt and pepper on each table. She was capturing one close to the door when she caught sight of a man sitting at an inside table by the window. He was looking her way, but she didn't know whether he was actually seeing her or not. It was scary how every man now seemed to look like Gary Adams. She knew it wasn't him, just a touch of paranoia on her part, but she zoomed in her lens anyway, just to be sure. However, once the focus cleared, the table was empty.

She knew she was being unreasonable, the city had over three hundred thousand inhabitants for heaven's sake, but suddenly it didn't seem like quite so nice a morning. She tucked the camera back into its case and walked the last two blocks more quickly. It was with relief that she mounted the steps, locked up her camera and gym bag, and went on in to exercise. A spinning class was about to start, so she signed the list on the door and went in. She thought it would feel good to burn away the fear with exercise. The instructor walked in, "Are we ready to kill it today?" Let the torture begin, Audrey thought.

An hour later, satisfied and dripping with sweat, Audrey sat in the small lounge area finishing her water. She'd refilled the bottle once and was still thirsty. It had been a great class, but what was it with these instructors? Did they hate people? She'd finished the last ten minutes on sheer pride alone, determined not to stop even though her body was screaming at her to. Oh well, she would survive. She packed everything up, leaving her camera in its case, and headed out the door, this time watching her surroundings more carefully as she made her way home. She didn't notice anyone who appeared to be watching her, so she shook off her nervousness and got ready to go to the service for Margot Pelletier.

Audrey had never attended the funeral service of someone from the police work she did. "Won't that be weird for me to be there?" She'd asked when Rod mentioned accompanying him.

"No, I don't think anyone will mind. Afterward, we can head down to the waterfront for dinner." He laughed. "It's a pretty strange start to a date, though. I'll give you that!"

Audrey laughed too, but since she'd begun to feel a real fondness for the woman, she'd agreed. He picked her up at three-thirty, and they arrived at the chapel in plenty of time to find a seat. Audrey looked around her at the small, intimate space and the few people who were gathering and wondered again about Margot Pelletier and her life. Why was it such a small crowd? As they walked up the steps, she saw the three Pelletier children standing side-by-side outside the doorway. The family resemblance was clear, all of them with straight, brown hair in varying shades and dark brown eyes. They greeted the detective by name as they shook hands, but Rod declined to introduce Audrey, and they stepped into the quiet chamber and took seats near the rear.

Rod leaned over to whisper to Audrey. "Sorry if I seemed rude back there, not introducing you to the family, but just in case it turns out one of them is a murderer, I don't think I want them to have your name."

Audrey hesitated, a bit shocked by his comment, before leaning in and whispering back. "Are you still considering that possibility?"

"I have to, at least for now. I've interviewed two out of the three, and so far, I can't find an alibi between them. It's the saddest set of circumstances I've seen in a while."

"Is that why this is such a small service? The three of them look so alone."

"I'm not sure what's going on. I think Mrs. Pelletier and her husband had real standing in the community, but the children don't seem to have many ongoing ties to the city. Perhaps the older family friends are gone or too infirm to attend. I don't know. Maybe they didn't want the publicity that a larger memorial service would bring."

"I guess I can understand wanting to keep it small and private." Before they could say any more, the adult children filed in and took their seats in the first pew. There was no casket in sight, just a photograph of the woman wearing a beautiful green top that suited her coloring and her crop of bright, white hair. She'd had a lovely smile, Audrey thought and wished again that she'd had an opportunity to meet her. A trio of singers added joy and beauty to the service, which celebrated rather than mourned the remarkable woman. Apparently, she had been quite a figure in the city's upper echelons, focusing her talents on development funding for the Carnegie Museums. Audrey was reminded that it had been much too long since she'd taken the opportunity to enjoy the culture available right in her own city.

After the service concluded, Audrey and Rod walked to his car and drove to one of the parking areas near the riverfront. They were planning on dinner downtown, but since it was still on the early side, they elected to go for a walk first. There were trees and flowers in bloom all around them, although many petals lay scattered on the sidewalk after the repeated rain showers that had marked the last few weeks. "Do you do any photography along the water here?" Rod asked as a group of cyclists pedaled by, more leisurely than many of the sets that typically whizzed around the city.

"I have. Especially as the weather gets nicer, more and more couples choose to do photoshoots with the riverwalk as a background. I've done a few engagement portraits here, as well as a sports-themed wedding that was down near the stadium."

"Hey, go Pirates, right?"

"Sorry, Steelers fans, not baseball." She paused, remembering the jacket she'd seen, and looked up at his face. "Are you a baseball fan?"

"Are you kidding me? Who doesn't like baseball? Summer afternoons, hot dogs in the stands. *If you build it, he will come,*" he intoned. "I love baseball." Rod paused briefly. "It reminds me of my dad, I guess. He was a huge fan, used to bet like crazy on every game. I still miss going with him." He turned to look at her. "No baseball fans in your family?"

"Nope, I grew up playing soccer. Lots more action, way fewer commercials."

"Well, I'll give you that. I get out to watch my nephew play whenever I can. He tried T-ball first, but it just didn't hold his interest."

"My parents have played in a softball league forever, and they swear that they beat younger teams not because they have more skill but because they have better attention spans."

"Oh, too right!" He laughed and took her hand as they continued to stroll.

Audrey was reminded again of how easy it was to talk with Rod, especially since they could cover topics that weren't associated with the work they shared. She was curious, though, about his comment on the Pelletier children. "So what did you mean about the Pelletiers not having any alibis? Are you convinced that she was pushed?"

"Oh no, nothing is convincing at all. That's what makes this so difficult. I can't even tell if there was a crime to begin with, but there's so much money involved that I can't rubber-stamp anything. I have to be sure."

"I figured they were all wealthy given the house. Aren't the children millionaires too?"

"Not as far as I can tell. I get the impression that Mr. And Mrs. Pelletier had to make their own way in the world, and they seem to have expected their children to do the same. The parents paid for their educations apparently, but none of them live extravagantly. Plus, they all three seem to have hit a tough spot at the same time. Did you notice anything at the service? Did anything seem off to you?"

"No, I didn't see anything out of the ordinary. That's rough, though, all of them having a bad time. I'm sorry to hear that. You look at an enormous house like that and think, everyone connected to it must be sitting pretty. I guess it's not always true, huh?"

"No, you're right. So, now on a lighter note, have you heard any more about that guy getting out of prison?"

"Lighter?" She chuckled uneasily. "I told my parents about it when I was home. You're going to think I'm being silly, but I could have sworn I saw him sitting in a coffee shop in my neighborhood this morning. How ridiculous is that?"

"Did you get a good look? Are you sure?"

She shook her head. "No, it was a quick glance, and then he was gone. I'm sure I'm being paranoid for no reason."

"Well, if you're ever afraid, please let me know. You have my number in your phone, right? And you carry it with you all the time?"

"Yep, I do. Listen, let's just let it go. I'm sure it was nothing. Are you starting to get hungry? I know it's still early, but I didn't eat much of a lunch."

"Sure, let's head back towards the restaurant. What are you hungry for?"

"Anything at this point."

"Anything?"

"Well, except for oysters. They're disgusting."

"Oh, my God, no baseball, no oysters. We have nothing in common! Can this relationship survive?" He flailed back in mock outrage and then pulled her against him in a quick hug before resuming their walk. Audrey thought she wouldn't have minded if it had turned into something more, but the night was still young.

24

Damn, his butt was numb. Gary Adams had awakened so early that he'd had to wait outside the coffee shop for it to open. Clearly, it was not a working-stiffs kind of place because they were all at work by now, and no working guys he knew were stupid enough to pay five dollars for a fuckin' cup of coffee. Now he'd been sitting in the place so long that he'd had to buy a second cup and a pastry so that the staff would quit glaring at him. He'd nearly finished the second cup and was thinking about shifting outdoors since the rain had stopped when he spotted her.

He wasn't sure it was her at first since she was holding a camera up in front of her face, but the build was right, and he knew that she was a photographer. He sat watching intently as she bent low, apparently focusing in on small things like flowers and weeds, cracks in the sidewalk for all he knew. It seemed stupid. But then she stood, checked behind her, and backed up against an old building before pointing her camera across the street at the shop where he was sitting. He sat very still studying her, not daring to move a muscle. He watched her lower the camera for a second before bringing it back up in front of her and turning the lens. He didn't think she'd seen him, but he knew a zoom lens when he saw one, and he stepped back and away from the table immediately.

From the corner of his eye, as he stood behind the wooden support for the doorway, he watched her adjusting the focus and then finally lowering the camera. He'd moved just in time. She packed her things up quickly after that, he noticed and took the slightest bit of satisfaction in the idea that perhaps he'd spooked her. Once she began walking again, he fell in behind her at a careful distance. She stopped at a sleek, modern building that was a poor fit with the surrounding area. It looked to be the fitness center, and he watched as both men and women scanned in key tags before entering.

Well, he thought, there was nothing else he could do there, so he turned the corner to see what was nearby. He considered sitting down again but caught sight of the small grocery store and opted to go in there instead. He figured it was worth checking to see if yesterday was a fluke or if she went there often enough for them to know her. He took his time walking around the three short aisles, looking at the ridiculous number of Asian products cramming the shelves. You couldn't even tell from the labels what most of the shit was. There was a slow, steady stream of customers, though, and he noted the woman in the red sari was nodding at several of them but not saying much. The man behind the counter, on the other hand, was a chatty Cathy if he'd ever seen one. It was like he thought he was the bartender at *Cheers* or something. Well, he'd be the target then. Gary picked up a can of soup and a few bananas and put on his friendliest mask.

"Good morning, sir." The clerk gave his head a slight bow. "How are you?"

"I'm good, thanks. This looks like a great place. Have you been here long?" The clerk looked over his shoulder at the older woman before answering.

"Yes, sir, nearly forty years now. Are you new to the neighborhood?"

"I am, yes. My friend Audrey Markum told me about this neighborhood, and I think I might have found a place. I'm meeting the realtor in just a few minutes."

"Oh, Audrey, what a wonderful young woman. She's in here quite often. Welcome to the neighborhood, Mr. . . . ." The clerk reached his hand over the counter, and Gary hesitated for what he hoped was just a fraction of a second before he gathered his thoughts and figured, what the hell? He'd use his own name. They wouldn't recognize it, but the bitch certainly would.

Shaking the clerk's hand he said, "Thank you. It's Gary, Gary Adams. Please tell her hello for me the next time she's in." Adams took the plastic bag and turned toward the door, risking one more look at the woman whose expression had not changed since he'd entered the market. Probably didn't even speak English, he thought, dismissing her from his mind. He figured he'd put in a good day so far, so he headed home. He'd have something to eat and decide what to do next.

25

Rod couldn't figure out exactly why he'd decided to ask Audrey to go with him to the Pelletier service. Oh, well, it wasn't worth psychologizing over it, as Smitty liked to put it. Especially since she looked lovely in the dark blue dress, she was wearing. He still needed to interview the younger son, but today didn't seem like the right time, so he'd made an appointment with him for the next morning. When Rod saw the Pelletier children lined up at the door, he had a moment of panic, wondering if he was taking Audrey to meet a murderer or two. He ushered her to their seats without pausing long enough for them to pay much attention to her, he hoped.

He watched the trio as they filed in and sat in the pew at the front. You wouldn't know they were each in such dire straits just to look at them. They looked fine, like normal, upright, sad funeral folks. Nothing stood out to him at all, and he wondered if Audrey saw anything more than he did. He was glad that they were going out afterward so that he could ask her what she noticed.

After the service, it felt good to get out and stretch his legs with Audrey. Once again, it had morphed from a wet, dark morning into a gloriously sunny afternoon. The sidewalks were busy with locals and tourists taking in the section of the riverfront where they were walking. Pittsburgh's history as a steel town had resulted in an odd legacy where city parks and landmarks, as well as neighborhoods and commercial areas, were located in and around the old sites of steel mills. Rod had been pleased when the new baseball stadium for his beloved Pirates opened down here, although he still regretted the fact that they hadn't named it after Clemente. Oh well, watching the old Three Rivers implode had been pretty damned exciting, too.

Rod had chosen a seafood restaurant nearby before he'd gotten the disturbing news that Audrey thought oysters were disgusting. He hoped there were other kinds of seafood that she liked. Jerome's had a good reputation, and without a game happening that night, he figured it'd be a little quieter than it was sometimes. The only cloud in the back of his mind was worry about Smitty. During the service, he'd had a quick text that the team had narrowed their focus in on two redneck brothers who had been at the dance club earlier in the evening and were seen fighting with some other dude's cousin. The team was watching the house and planning to move on them anytime. It was a challenge for Rod, not checking his phone constantly or calling to see what was up. He'd rather keep his attention on Audrey, and he knew that Smitty wouldn't appreciate the distraction if something happened, but it was weighing in the back of his mind.

Throughout dinner, he was reminded of the difference between talking to Smitty's sister when they were dating and talking to Audrey. She seemed to have an interest in so many different things that they moved easily between topics. He loved the matter-of-fact way Audrey approached things as well as how quick she was to laugh. He could remember hearing his mom and dad up late at night, laughing together in the kitchen at the old house. Until he heard Audrey's quick laugh tonight, he hadn't realized how much he'd been missing that.

After dinner, they began walking back to the car just as Rod's phone buzzed. It was Smitty. "Do you mind?" He looked up at Audrey.

"Of course not."

He thumbed in the code and saw the terse note from his partner. *Moving in, wish us luck.* He said a quick prayer in his mind before pocketing the phone and taking Audrey's hand.

"Trouble?" She asked.

"Sorry, it's work. My partner is on an assignment tonight. He was just checking in."

"Have you two been working together long?"

"About three years, maybe? Full confession, I was seeing Smitty's sister for quite some time, but we broke it off a while back."

"No hard feelings with him?"

"No, none, zippo, turned out when we weren't getting along, both of us were complaining to him and making *him* miserable. We've all been better off since that ended. He's a great partner, and I'm anxious about tonight. They think they've found the guys from the dance club."

"Wow, so soon."

"Well, the bigger the asshole, the bigger the talk sometimes. These clowns didn't leave much to the imagination. They're idiots, but dangerous ones."

Rod was glad when they reached the car and drove back to her place. The summer construction season seemed to be getting into full sway early, and their path was a circuitous one that took a third longer than it usually would.

"Don't you love the city in the spring? The beautiful orange cones and the bright green safety vests?" Audrey teased.

He shook his head. Making fun of it was probably the best approach, and he appreciated her take on it. He was thinking about routes blocked and emergency locations, but he forced himself to knock it off. He was on a date, for God's sake, not on duty. "Oh yeah, two of my favorite colors, definitely!"

"There's no parking lot for my building, so this may be as close as we can get." Audrey gestured at a parking space a block down from her apartment. He parked and suddenly remembered the gentleman thing and went around to open her door. Of course, she was already climbing out by then, but he figured, points for thinking of it. When they reached her building, he watched her key in the short code for the outer door.

"Well, that's just pathetic." He gestured above them at the burned-out light.

"What?"

"You've got a half-assed code that probably half a million people know and one light over the door that's not even working."

Audrey pulled open the door and then led the way into her unit. "I know. I emailed the landlord about the light when I noticed it yesterday.

Come on in. I'll show you my deadbolt!" He was happy to see the security she had on her unit, but the whole setup bothered him anyway. He did not like knowing that Adams could be out there in the city somewhere, possibly keeping tabs on her.

"Do you want some coffee or juice? I'm afraid I'm out of beer and wine and, you know, most regular food." He looked over her shoulder at the nearly empty refrigerator.

"Jeez Louise, you're as bad as me. I think I have half a sandwich and some dog food in my fridge. We're pitiful."

"You know what's even worse?"

"What?"

She lowered her head before bringing it up, laughing. "The juice I have is in little boxes."

"Okay, you win. That is way worse than me. Why in the hell do you have juice boxes, may I ask? You don't appear to be a ten-year-old soccer player anymore."

She punched him in the stomach gently before turning to make a fresh pot of coffee. He leaned against the short counter and waited for the coffee grinder to stop before saying anything more.

"Well, my juice may be in boxes, but my coffee is excellent," Audrey bragged. He could smell it already and knew that she was telling the truth. "Let's sit down while we wait for it."

"Or maybe we could do this instead?" He pulled her to him and lowered his mouth to hers. After two short kisses, he paused. "I have wanted to do that all day." Then he pulled her closer to him and loved the way she fit, not too tall, not too short, just perfect. They continued their embrace minutes after the coffee pot had offered its small ding, but then he felt his phone buzz in his pocket. Immediately his mind was back on Smitty. He took a step back. "I'm sorry, one second." Audrey moved to the cabinet and pulled down two mugs while he checked the phone. The message was from his lieutenant. "*Smitty hit, at Mercy, touch and go.*"

"Oh, God, I have to go."

"What's wrong?"

"Smitty's been shot. He's at Mercy. I gotta go."

"Oh no, I mean yes. Go. Go." She grabbed up his jacket but held it against her for a brief moment. "Please let me know what happens. No matter when. I'm going to be worried."

He kissed her once more and then took the jacket and fished his keys out of the pocket. "I will."

26

A light was flashing brightly, and it pulled Audrey from sleep. She'd set the alarm for her phone and left it charging near her bed so that she wouldn't miss a call from Rod about his partner. The text said. *"He's doing better. Lost a lot of blood. I'm here donating and plan to stay until morning. Last night was terrific. I'm sorry I had to cut it short."* She breathed a sigh of relief and fell back against her pillow. It was three AM. She typed a quick response. *"Thanks for letting me know, was worried. Will come down to donate in the morning."*

Audrey gave herself an hour to fall back to sleep and was about to give up when she turned and realized her alarm was going off. By now, the bedroom had begun to fill with light. So she'd fallen back to sleep after all. She got up and showered quickly, throwing on jeans and a light-weight top for the day. She wanted to pick up some things at the market before heading over to the hospital to donate blood. This time she took her pack and a couple of bags, figuring she'd call for a ride if it turned out to be too much to schlep home on foot. She was hoping that Rod would come to dinner that night, and she wanted to have some actual food to offer him.

When she got to the market, she picked out one of the wheeled carts and saw Mrs. Patel raise her eyebrows at her. "Company coming!" Audrey called to her and continued to move along the aisle. She tried to remember if Mrs. Patel had ever actually spoken to her in the past. Audrey wasn't sure she had, although her face communicated *a lot* of information. Audrey often thought that Sunan looked a little afraid of her sometimes. Audrey finished locating the ingredients for a simple dinner and stopped by the counter, looking into the pastry case, wondering just what she should splurge on for dessert.

Sunan walked over and stood, waiting to open the back of the cabinet. "Morning, Miss Audrey. How are you?"

"I'm good, Sunan. I think I'm going to opt for the rice pudding, please." She looked around her. "Did I miss the baby?"

"Oh, no, my son is bringing her around in about half an hour if you can wait."

"Oh, I wish I could, but I need to get these things home and get moving."

"It was delightful to meet your friend yesterday."

She looked at him quizzically, wondering who in the world he might have meant. Had Rod been by here yesterday? "Who is that, Sunan?"

"He was a man, about my age? He said you'd told him good things about the neighborhood. He said his name was Gary Adams."

Audrey felt her body stop, as though a door had opened and an icy draft had forced her to catch her breath. She looked from Sunan to Mrs. Patel but couldn't figure out what to say.

"Is something wrong?" Sunan asked as he rang up the items and placed them in her bags. Then Mrs. Patel walked over and stood beside her son-in-law.

"He wasn't a friend, was he?" She asked in beautifully accented English. Audrey shook her head.

Sunan turned to look at his mother-in-law. "How could you tell?"

"It was the eyes." She turned from Sunan to Audrey. "His eyes didn't match what he was saying."

"I have to go," Audrey spoke finally, but it came out as more of a whisper. She pocketed her card, slipped into her backpack, and positioned the bags on her shoulders.

"Sunan, walk her home." Mrs. Patel looked at Audrey as she spoke, but Audrey wasn't comfortable making him leave the store.

"No, it's okay. I'm fine. He's just someone I knew a long time ago. I'll be okay. I'm going to take these things right home and then head to the hospital to see a friend. I'll get a ride there."

"Are you sure?" Sunan asked, pausing before re-tying his apron.

Audrey felt like she didn't have enough spit left to say much more, so she nodded and took off quickly. With her backpack and a bag slung over each shoulder, she was able to make surprisingly good time. She kept her head on a swivel, as her dad called it, and keyed in the outer door's lock code as quickly as she could. Once inside, she slammed her lock home and called for the ride even before putting away the groceries.

When her ride texted that he was downstairs, she stopped for a moment to look out the window by her sink, studying the sidewalk and cars below her unit. She could see the dark blue Honda that matched the make and model given in her app, but she still paused at the bottom of the stairs, double-checking what the driver looked like and making sure that no other cars were lurking nearby. Once settled in the backseat, she kept a careful watch on the area around her building as they pulled away.

It didn't take her long to get to Mercy Hospital or to find the crowd of blue uniforms milling around in the lobby. She spoke to the first policeman that she recognized and learned that Smitty wasn't the only officer who'd been shot in the raid. The other man, a uniform with only two years under his belt, was in worse shape than Rod's partner. Just then, Rod stepped out from around the corner, and it took every bit of will that Audrey had not to throw herself into his arms and spill out what had happened at the market. But it could wait. This couldn't.

"How is he doing?"

"Better, his sister's with him now, so I decided to make myself scarce. I came to usher the next group down to donate blood."

"I'd like to do that too, can I?"

"Sure, come with me." He gestured two other uniforms after them, and the group headed down one hallway after another until it felt as if they must be in another building by now. Perhaps they were. The blood center was long and narrow, with two rows of beds and at least three nurses on staff. Clearly, they were used to the blue flood of volunteers that came with any first responder injuries. Audrey took the chair on the end, allowing the others to go first.

Rod kneeled down next to her. "Listen, I can't stay right now. Can I give you a call later? I appreciate you coming down. It means a lot to me."

Audrey reached out to hold his hands. "Could you come for dinner tonight? I bought some actual food, but I need to talk to you about something, too."

"Sure, I'd love that. Is six too early if I can get away?"

"No, that'll be perfect. Thank you and be careful. I'll see you tonight."

Rod ducked in for a quick kiss. "Tonight then." And he was off. Audrey felt safe in the hospital and was in no hurry to get back to her neighborhood. Two more officers appeared at the door, and she let all of them go ahead of her. She thought about texting her mother and father, but there was a big 'No Cell Phones' sign on the wall across from her, so she made a quick check for messages and then put it away.

In the end, she opted to let all of the uniforms go before her. It was interesting enough watching the group. Some seemed to know each other and paired up to wait their turn while others kept to themselves, sitting quietly, sometimes with their eyes closed. Audrey wondered how many of them were there because they knew the injured men and how many were there just because it was the right thing to do. Either way, the blood would be helpful for a lot of patients, not simply the police officers. Audrey was embarrassed to tell the intake nurse that she had donated blood only once before, at a blood drive back in college. She took her time looking through the required reading materials and then returned to the desk to have a blood sample taken and her blood pressure checked. When both were given the go-ahead, Audrey was left with a laptop to answer the long list of pre-donation questions. She moved her chair to signal when she had completed it, and the nurse finished the intake quickly.

A few old magazines were left on the table against the wall, so Audrey picked one up on her way to the bed. She wasn't terribly edgy about blood and needles, but she figured it couldn't hurt to have a distraction. The nurses were skilled at their job, though, and Audrey had little to be concerned about. Once she finished, she watched as the site was bandaged and was surprised to see that there was almost no mark at all. Audrey was led to a small kitchenette then and sat with the last two officers as they all had a snack and drink before heading out. One of them, a big, burly man with salt and pepper hair, looked almost comical as he ate the bag of miniature cookies. He took his time picking them up one by one, but the tiny bag seemed so inadequate that Audrey was about to comment when she noticed that the current bag was resting on a pile of three or four empty ones. Okay, she thought, guess he'll survive.

She opened the can of juice and selected her own bag of miniature cookies. She pictured the fear on Rod's face as he'd told her about his partner and said a small prayer that the donations that day would be of use.

Rod hated to leave the hospital, but with Smitty's family there, he felt like he was leaving him in good hands. He told himself it wasn't because of the awkwardness around Smitty's sister. It was a little bit, he guessed, not because there were any feelings left between them, but perhaps because there weren't. How could they have dated for so long and not ended up with a stronger connection between the two of them, he wondered? An image of Audrey sitting in the line to donate blood slipped into his mind, and the rush of feelings was almost overwhelming. None of it made sense, he thought, at least not to an amateur like himself. He drove to the precinct, eager to focus his mind on something other than his love life.

The office seemed to be buzzing with activity when he got there, but most of it turned out to be a rehashing of the night's events rather than any new action. The shooters had all been involved in the firefight, the red-necked brothers as well as the cousin, and there was considerable anger that the men had come out of it with few injuries. But, with the bastards now in custody, there was little more for the team to do than the three R's, as Rod and Smitty called it--recount, rethink, and regret. It seemed that every after-hours drinking party they went to included those three elements, the storytelling and the second-guessing that they all hated but were also helpless to stop. Rod walked past it all and sat down at his desk, throwing headphones on as he sat down to type up and go over the interviews he'd done so far regarding Mrs. Pelletier's death. Jules Pelletier, the middle child, was expected in half an hour, and Rod wanted to be sure that he was ready.

After he typed up what he'd gotten from the other two, he took a few minutes to go back over the report from the forensic team and look through Audrey's photographs. He paged through them on his computer screen, flipping past some while scrutinizing others. But nothing seemed any more straightforward than when he started. If he could just figure out what it was that had gotten the older woman out of bed at that early hour. He'd reviewed the phone records for her cell as well as the landline but had turned up nothing. In the weeks before her death, she had received calls from all three of her children, but then they'd told him that much already. When he looked back further, it seemed as though Mrs. Pelletier had been speaking with all three of her children at least once or twice a week for several months. He wondered if that was normal, an indication of how close they were, or was it more to do with the recent difficulty that each of them had fallen into? Once Smitty was feeling better, he thought he'd ask him and Audrey about how often they talked with their folks. Having lost his father when he was in his late teens and his mother a year ago, Rod needed a point of reference. Maybe they could give him something to compare it to. He also wondered if any one of Mrs. Pelletier's staff knew her well enough to be aware of the calls and if they were normal or not. He wrote himself a note to ask them about that. He was curious how much the staff knew about the woman's private life.

When Jules Pelletier arrived just after one o'clock, Rod thought he looked like an 'after' version of his brother. Put the first one on a healthy diet, remove the alcohol and clean him up, and you'd have this one. Jules was trim and athletic where Arnaud had been starting to soften. He also seemed to be a lot more tightly wrapped. What was the same, though, across all three of them were their sad, brown eyes. Jules's were the darkest and made an interesting contrast to the close-cropped light brown hair. "Sit, please. Thank you for coming in." Rod stood and shook Jules's hand and then gestured him into the chair and sat again himself. "How are you doing, Mr. Pelletier? I thought the service was very nice. Your mother seems to have been quite a woman."

"Thank you, Detective, she was. We appreciated your coming to the service." He offered no more, so Rod began his questioning.

"You understand, Mr. Pelletier, that although the body was released for burial, the case is still not closed. I spoke with your brother and sister about their whereabouts last week, and now I'd like to hear about yours. When did you arrive in Pittsburgh?"

Jules sat very straight in his chair and spoke carefully. "I came into town on Wednesday afternoon last week for a job interview."

"And where was that?"

"It was at a dental practice on the northeast side of the city. I can give you their name and address if I have to, although I'm sure you can see what an awkward position that would put me in."

"Were you planning to move to the city?" Rod watched as Jules pressed the fingertips of both hands together, and he wondered if it was some sort of stress reduction strategy. If so, it didn't seem to be helping much, as he could hear the strain in the man's voice when he replied.

"Detective, I'm sure you've done your homework on all of us and know all about what happened at my practice in Buffalo. My wife and sons have been through a lot this past year, and we thought it would be good to change things up. I am licensed in both New York state and Pennsylvania, and, with my mother getting older and needing more care, my wife and I were considering moving here to make a fresh start for ourselves as well as to help her."

"You were planning to live there at the house?"

Jules tilted his head slightly. "Temporarily, yes, while we looked for a place. The costs are much higher here than at home, so we wanted to give ourselves time to look carefully before jumping into renting or buying a place."

"So what time was the interview over, and what did you do after that?"

"The interview finished just before five o'clock. I got in my car but was hesitant to get out into the evening commuter traffic. After all, I didn't have to be anywhere by any particular time."

"You weren't meeting your brother or sister?"

"No, we planned to meet for dinner on Thursday evening. I was hoping to share my ideas with them when we got together."

"All right, so you're in your car . . ."

"I called my wife, and we had a long discussion about the interview and the prospect of moving here. She was more hesitant than I was about the plan since she is from New York, and this move would take her farther away from her family. She is also concerned because our twin sons will be starting high school this fall, and she doesn't like the idea of moving them away from their friends."

"Sounds like it's been a tough sell."

"Yes, in a word, yes it has. We had hoped that once the trial finished, everything would calm down at home. I had even toyed with the idea of opening my own practice there, but I don't have the funds for it."

"So then your mother's money would have come in pretty handy, wouldn't it? Everyone could stay in Buffalo where they're happy, and you'd have the funds you need to get started on your own."

Jules jumped to his feet, and Rod quickly rested his hand on his firearm as the man picked up the chair and slammed it back down. With the sound, Jules seemed to come back to himself and noticed the alarm on Rod's face and the uniformed officer who had stepped up behind him. In an instant, his shoulders sagged, and he held his hands up in front of him defensively. "I'm sorry, so sorry. I didn't mean to lose my temper that way." Rod lifted his chin in a brief nod that indicated that he had things under control, and the policeman turned back to what he'd been doing. "I'm sorry, I've just spent months having to defend myself from people making all kinds of claims--that I was hurting patients too or, at best, turning a blind eye to what was going on around me. But I was just busy doing my work, being a dentist, for God's sake. I never saw anything wrong. I thought my partner was an honorable man. Detective, I'm sure I must be both stupid and naïve, but I swear to you, I am not a criminal of any kind. I love my mother." He paused before changing the verb tense and lowering his voice. The tension in it seemed to melt into sorrowfulness. "I loved my mother dearly, and although my wife was hesitant, I knew that moving in with my mother for a bit would have been a good step to take. She was a bright, caring woman with a keen head for business. I would much rather have her advice and support than her money, believe me."

"All right, I hear that. So you're in your car talking to your wife. Then what?"

"I hung up and turned on the radio to catch a traffic report. I was north of the river, and the place my sister had rented for Thursday was on the south side. I'd been planning on staying at a hotel somewhere down there, but the roads were terrible. An accident earlier inside one of the tunnels had slowed everything down, and it was total hash. I found a couple of restaurants nearby on my phone, so I got out of the car and walked a few blocks. The first one I came to had gone out of business, but the second one was open, so I had some dinner."

"And after that? What time did you finish?"

"I guess it was about seven-thirty or eight. I had canceled my hotel reservation earlier when I realized I wasn't going to make it given the state of the traffic, so I started checking on what was available close by. Turns out, there aren't as many hotels up on that side of the city. I had to drive almost ten miles back out of town to find a place. They said they had a room when I called, so I headed that way, but by the time I got there, the room was taken. Mothers' Day business, I suppose."

Oh, good Lord, Rod thought. This idiot isn't going to have an alibi either. He looked at him and waited for him to finish his tale of woe. "Really?"

Jules looked up at Rod and then closed his eyes briefly before resuming his fingertip push-up routine. He looked up at the detective finally. "Really. I was just off the highway, so I got back on and pulled off at a rest area. I went inside and used the facilities, then came back out and slept in my car. I was beat."

Rod shook his head back and forth slowly as he doodled on a legal pad. He seemed to be drawing a series of circles within circles, which was precisely what was happening with the damn case. "So who can verify that story, Mr. Pelletier? Did you speak to anyone? Have you got any receipts?"

"Well, sure." He pulled out a brown leather wallet and opened it to reveal the bill's section filled with neatly folded receipts. "I always get a receipt." He laid them out one by one. "This is the restaurant. This is the rest stop. This is gas at the rest stop."

Rod looked at each one. They were easy to read with three matching signatures, but the latest timestamp was right before midnight. He looked over at Jules. "The latest one is 11:54, Mr. Pelletier. Your mother died between three and four in the morning. You see the problem here, right?"

"What about the calls to my wife?"

"From a cell phone, right? Listen, Mr. Pelletier. Tell me, what do you think happened to your mother? Why was she up at that hour of the night and going downstairs? Were you there? Did you maybe give her a little push, get that money for your new practice?" Rod had seen suspects go pale before, but he wasn't sure he'd seen anyone go quite this white, at least not someone who was still alive. It looked as if Jules was starting to sway, and suddenly Rod was afraid the man was going to puke all over his desk. He grabbed the waste can and pulled it over close. Pelletier closed his eyes, swallowed a few times, and began pushing his fingertips together again much more vigorously as he fought to maintain control. Finally, he seemed to pull himself back from whatever brink he'd been teetering on, and Rod set the trash can back down.

"I thought I'd heard the worst when I was in Buffalo. I was wrong. I'm going to go now. I need to call my lawyer. Please let me know when you need to speak to me again, and I'll make an appointment for her to join us." Rod stood and watched as Jules tucked the chair neatly into place and walked slowly toward the front door. He thought there was still a chance that the man might faint or puke, but he managed to make it out under his own steam.

Well damn, now what? Rod thought as he collapsed back down into his chair. Three people about to inherit fortunes and not a credible alibi among them. He tried to parse out a way where the three of them might be in cahoots, some weird *Murder on the Orient Express* deal, or something, but nothing came to him. He entered his notes into the case file and shut down the computer. Then he made a call over to the hospital and learned that both men had improved while he'd been busy interviewing the third stooge. At least that was good news, and he had dinner to look forward to.

CHAPTER
28

Adams couldn't believe his luck when he found a sublet right in the little bitch's neighborhood. He had seen the 3x5 card advertising it the day before when he'd been watching from the coffee shop. He'd been standing near the entrance waiting when a messy bulletin board caught his eye. The second-floor apartment was in a duplex practically across the street from her building, and because it was just for a month, he could afford the ridiculous rent.

He'd used the computers at the library to dummy up a letter of reference and then emailed a copy of it to the apartment owner. It wouldn't have borne up to any kind of scrutiny, but the idiot owner was so eager, so stupid and trusting he'd never even checked on it. He'd just accepted the envelope of cash and handed over the keys. Since the bouncer job had come with the offer of a small advance and a solid lead on a handgun, Adams felt he had everything he needed. Now, he was sitting pretty right across the street from that bitch. It made him happy seeing how agitated and anxious she'd been, walking home with all of those bags, a look of panic on her face as she constantly scanned the area around her.

After seeing how edgy she had been coming home from the market, Adams was surprised at how quickly she came back out. But this time, there was a car waiting for her and no opportunity for him to act. He had picked up some more groceries of his own, so he took his time preparing some lunch for himself and then eating while he watched the monstrous flat-screen TV that hung in the apartment's small living room. It seemed to take up half the space. He loved it. The owner had purchased some sort of sports package, so Adams was able to view one game after another without having to sit through any of the worthless bullshit that his wife used to like to watch.

Adams kept an eye out the window and saw when Audrey was being dropped off in front of her building. He watched her key in the outside code. He'd only had to watch two or three people do it before he'd mastered it—some security, what a joke. Right now, though, he was enjoying the TV too much to bother getting up. Instead, he waited through a long string of commercials, figuring out just what he would do, how he would capture her, and then what he'd do with her once he had her. He'd watched her routine enough to guess that she would be going out to the gym in the morning. He figured that would be his best opportunity for catching her by surprise. She'd never know he was there.

It was closer to dinner time when he saw a car park down on the street, and a man get out and go to the door of her apartment building. He caught a glimpse of Audrey then as she opened the door and ushered him in. Gary looked at the man's car again and noted the light fixed to the top of it. Goddamn, she was seeing a cop? What were the chances of that? He'd have to keep checking to see if the car stayed the night so that he'd know whether or not she would be alone in the morning. Adams pulled a pan of lasagna out of the freezer and started it heating while he watched the last few minutes of the baseball game and planned his next move.

29

Audrey was tired by the time the car let her out in front of her apartment, not just from the blood draw but from the night's tension and the revelation at the market. She wanted to curl up on the sofa and do nothing, but Rod was coming over, and she wanted to be able to offer him a good meal. She thought about calling her mom to talk about it or, even better, her friend Katy. She'd had a text that Katy was back and that the future in-laws had not been nearly as frightening as she had feared. Audrey hated to burst her friend's happy bubble, though, and she knew that her mother would worry and tell her to come home. That would not be helpful either. Maybe it was just that telling Rod about it seemed like the most prudent step to take. He would know what she should do. She was relying on it.

Although she'd always loved watching her dad cook, Audrey had not learned as much from him as she had hoped. Luckily, he had gifted her with a handwritten cookbook of her favorite meals when she graduated from college. His chili was one recipe that she'd learned and even improved on, so that was what she planned to make. She also had the materials for a good salad and a bag of crusty rolls that she loved from the market. She put on some music and got to work. By five o'clock, with nearly everything ready, she had time to rest. The salad was stored in the refrigerator, and the chili could simmer happily until Rod arrived. It just needed a stir now and again. She figured she'd use the time to start working her way through the photos from Jeff and Jerry's wedding.

Before sitting down, she set the timer on the stove for ten minutes so that she could bury herself in her work but not forget to get up and stir the chili. First, she took her time looking through the formal poses and comparing them to the list that she'd been given before the ceremony. Jeff's mother was a little nervous and squinty-eyed in many of them, but Audrey was able to sift through and find a good number that she felt everyone would be happy with. She set up the folder and files where everything would be stored until the package was complete, and she was ready to meet with the couple. The timer dinged. Audrey got up and stirred the pot, then reset the timer and got to work again. Midway through her second work period, her phone vibrated in her pocket.

"Hi, Mom, what's up?" Audrey asked, walking back into the kitchen as she talked. She began collecting the plates and bowls for dinner, trying to be as quiet as possible as she did it.

"It's Sandy, hon." Her mother said, a cheerful tone to her voice. "I just had a call from her mother. She went into labor this afternoon."

"Wait, it's early, isn't it? Is everything okay? What time did she go in? When did her mom call?"

"Oh, I think everything is all right. Twins often come a little bit early. I just got off the phone with her mom and called you right away. Cecelia was going to head over and keep her company while they wait for Sandy's husband to get there from work."

"He isn't far away, is he?"

"Oh, no, no, Oscar was just over near Butler. It took them a little while to get through to his cell, is all. He's heading over to meet them at the hospital now."

Audrey looked at the pot bubbling away on her stove. "Should I come too, do you think?" She reached toward the knob for the burner as she spoke.

"Uh-uh. Sandy forbade anyone else from coming to the hospital. She says she's frightened enough as it is and doesn't want a bunch of people hanging around making her more nervous than she already is."

Audrey gave the big pot another stir and pictured her friend Sandy as she was in high school, her face and body in a total panic as they prepared for prom together. "I can picture her saying that!"

"I plan to give her mother a call before we turn in for bed tonight and see how things are going. I'll text you with what I hear."

"Okay, Mom, I appreciate that. I'll call you back in the morning, and we can make a plan to go and see them once they're ready for us tomorrow."

"Sounds good, honey. I'll talk to you in the morning!"

Audrey reset her kitchen timer but had more difficulty falling back into her work this time. She'd known Sandy forever, it seemed. Granted, they hadn't been as close lately as they had been in elementary and high school, but they'd continue to check in with each other fairly often during their years at college. Audrey was happy she'd poked her head in on Sunday. For a moment, she wondered if their roles would ever be reversed. She tried imagining herself holding a newborn, but the picture wasn't coming into focus very well. She was still in her twenties, though, and nothing was going to push her into something until she was ready for it. Being with the rat bastard, Charlie, had taught her that much. She didn't plan to put blinders on ever again. Audrey loved weddings and loved photographing them, but so far, it hadn't made her hunger for her own. At least not yet.

She looked at the clock again and then over at her laptop. She probably wasn't going to get anything more done on the photographs today, so she shut down the files and killed time playing a game of solitaire before closing it up. She set out the two placemats and dishes that matched and was reaching for glasses when her phone vibrated again. It was a text from Rod, "*On my way now.*" She finished setting the small table and went to use the bathroom and freshen up. She was setting the rolls out, ready to warm in the oven, when the front door buzzed, and she went to let him in.

He scooped her into a quick, unexpected hug before putting her down and following her into the room. She was surprised at how good it felt. "It smells amazing in here, Audrey. What's for dinner?"

"I made my dad's chili. Come on in." She hung his light jacket on the hook by the door and led him over to the small kitchen. She pointed toward the nearest stool before reaching for the refrigerator door. "I now have beer, soda, wine, and water. What would you like?" She gestured with a small flourish.

"A beer would be great, thanks. How do you feel since you gave blood today?"

"A little tired but otherwise okay. How're Smitty and the other officer doing?"

"Better, it's such a relief. Smitty and I've been working together for so long that he feels like the brother I never had. It was hard thinking we might lose him, especially since I wasn't there when it all went down."

"I'm glad he's doing better, but selfish me is also glad that you weren't there. Did the shooting keep you busy all day today?" Audrey turned the burner off and tucked the rolls into the oven for a few minutes before coming to sit beside him on the other stool.

"No, the guys who were responsible for it are all in custody, so there wasn't anything for me to do. I spent my afternoon interviewing the last of the Pelletiers. Jeez, what a family for bad luck. Do you think it runs like that, luck? Sometimes I wonder."

"I guess I never thought about it much. What makes them so unlucky?"

"Aw, man, they were all planning to move home, for one reason or another. I don't know if the old woman knew that or not."

"All three of her children?"

"Yup, one crisis after another and not a damned alibi between them. They've all got access to the place, they all seemed to know about the shitty elevator, any one of them could have gotten in and out, and no one would be the wiser."

"But do you know for sure that Mrs. Pelletier was pushed?"

"Nope, and that's the kicker. They're all desperate for money, and here's the easy solution handed to them on a silver platter. Any one of them had reason enough to want to speed up her demise. But I'm damned if I can tell whether they did or not. If I could only figure out what got her out of bed at that hour, I might have a clue. You haven't thought of anything, have you?"

"No, sorry. I haven't. What are you going to do?"

"Well, tomorrow I'm going to go back out and talk to the staff one more time and see if I can get any sense as to how the woman felt about her children coming home, either to visit or to stay. I want to hear from them about what worries or concerns they think Mrs. Pelletier might have had about the three of them."

"Sounds like a good idea." Audrey hopped up and went over to the stove. She picked up the deep ladle and scooped out two servings. "Here, take this bowl and grab your beer. It's not much of a table, but it beats sitting on those high stools. My feet go numb if I sit there too long." Once she'd set the second bowl on the table, she retrieved the salad from the refrigerator and tossed it with the dressing she'd made. She put that on the table, then retrieved the rolls and toppled them into a napkin-lined basket that she'd set by the stove. "This is it, then. I hope you like it!"

Rod stood and waited while she took her seat before pulling out the other chair and sitting down himself. "Why don't we take a break from police talk tonight? I'm about done in thinking about it all. I'd like to leave it until tomorrow, that is unless you can solve it for me, Scout?"

"No way, not tonight. I have no official thoughts on the matter. I can tell you something nice, though."

"Oh, what's that?"

"My friend Sandy from the old neighborhood is having twins right now."

"Really? That's amazing. I have no idea how anyone could handle two babies at the same time. I watched my sister's son a few times when he was a baby, and I couldn't believe how hard it was."

"I don't know how she'll do it either, but her mom and her husband are both great, so she'll have a lot of support." Audrey hesitated, fully aware that it was entirely too early to ask such a loaded question, but she did it anyway. If it scared him off, that would be useful information to have. "So, do you want to have kids? Or I guess I should ask if you have any kids already."

At least he didn't choke on his chili, she thought. "No, I don't have any children, but I would like some one day. I don't think I'm ready for all of that yet, but I figure I have time. And you?" He looked around them. "No little ones in the background here?"

"Nope, not so far. I was dating a guy for a long while, and I thought it might go somewhere, but . . ."

"But?"

"He fell for a woman in his office. Took his time telling me about it, which was super sweet, you know. I've been a little gun-shy, I guess you'd say. You're the first person I've been out with since then. It's nice." She smiled over at him as she handed him the basket of rolls. "Oops, I forgot the butter. One second." She was glad to have the distraction, given the intensity of the conversation. Once she returned, she was able to relax as he fell into telling a funny story about his dog Simon and how he'd earned his name. It was such a pleasant conversation that it was more than an hour later before she remembered to tell him about Gary Adams.

"Oh no, I forgot what I needed to tell you. I've been totally freaked out about it all day, and here you made me forget it all. Thank you."

"What's got you freaked out?"

"I went to the corner market this morning to get the things for dinner, and when I was talking to the owner and her son-in-law, they told me that a man named Gary had chatted them up and talked about how he was old friends with me."

"Gary? Gary who?"

Audrey took a deep breath. "He gave his name. It was Gary Adams. Fresh out of prison and for some reason, in my particular neighborhood."

Rod pushed back from the table in a sudden movement and went to his jacket to retrieve his phone. "Did you tell anyone? Report it?"

"Who would I report it to? What would I even say? That some guy in a market told people that he knew me? I'd sound like a lunatic. Besides, to be honest, once I was home safely, I didn't feel like talking to anyone but you about it. What do you think I should do?"

Rod looked over at her door. "I like your deadbolt, for starters. But we need to talk to the landlord about that pathetic lock on the outside. Can you give me their contact information?"

"Sure, I'll get it when we're done. But Rod, that's going to inconvenience a lot of people just for me."

"Who cares? They'll all be safer if it's taken care of, not just you. Would you rather handle it than have me do it?"

"I'd like to try. I've called about it before, but I'll put my foot down this time and give the landlord your name and number if I feel like they're not taking me seriously. What else should I do? I can't just hide in here. I have to be able to work. I've got a rehearsal dinner to shoot tomorrow night and a brunch and wedding on Sunday. Plus, I could get called out by your office at some point, too."

He was busy typing on his phone, so Audrey paused, dipping her roll into the sauce on the edge of her bowl. She took a small bite and then set it back down, her appetite gone. "Okay, I just sent a message through a few channels to find out what kind of supervision he's supposed to be under and if there's a parole officer assigned. Stalking you could easily land him back inside. Now let's think about the next few days. How do you get around in the city? You said you don't have a car, right?"

"Right, I take the bus a lot in the winter. My dad offered me his old bug, but it was such a pain to park and dig out of the snow that I gave it back. He finally donated it last year. Usually, if it's not too far and if it doesn't matter how I look, I walk or bike to where I'm going, especially now that the weather's getting so nice."

"How predictable are you?"

"What do you mean?"

"You mentioned the market, right? Where else do you walk regularly?"

"The gym's the only other place I go to often other than the coffee shop where we met, but that isn't as frequent."

"Do you have a usual time you go to the gym?"

Audrey dropped her hands into her lap before wringing them together in fear. "I usually go first thing in the morning, around eight, if I can."

"Well, that right there will need to change. We don't want anything you're doing to be predictable. So what about other times when you don't want to walk? For weddings, say?"

"Then I call a car service or a cab depending on the timing and how far I have to go."

"Hm, that's a little more challenging. Everyone tries to scope out their drivers, but it's not foolproof. Okay, let's just think one day at a time here. What's on your schedule for tomorrow?"

"Well, I was planning to go to the gym first thing so that I'd be free when my mom calls. She's planning to pick me up so that we can go and visit Sandy and the babies. Then I'm due at a downtown hotel for a rehearsal dinner. They just wanted a few shots from the beginning, so I'm not expecting to be out too late. What am I going to do?"

Rod stood and dropped his phone back into his jacket pocket. Then he came back to the table and took Audrey's hand, pulling her up to face him. "First," he leaned in and kissed her, then tilted his head back slightly. "We're not going to let any of this ruin our evening. This is a fantastic dinner, and I want us to enjoy it. We can figure out tomorrow together." He leaned back in, and Audrey felt herself melting against him. It was the safest and most relaxed she'd felt since she'd left Sunan and Mrs. Patel at the market that morning. She wrapped her hands around his back and held tight. They would figure it out later.

CHAPTER

30

Rod was startled out of a deep sleep by a strobing light and an insistent buzzing, neither of which he could identify. It felt a little like being back in his old black and white cruiser, but the light wasn't quite right. He heard a voice then and felt a body shift beside him on the bed. "Sorry, I forgot I had set my alarm for so early." Ah, it was Audrey. He felt her reaching to turn off the alarm and then noticed the early morning light filtering in around the edges of the curtain. He pulled her in next to him, her slim hips fitting against him so perfectly. He thought he'd been wildly optimistic bringing two condoms with him to dinner. Now he was wishing he'd brought a third. Audrey had confessed to throwing out her supply after Charlie's exit, so there was nothing to do but enjoy the warmth of her and think about next time.

"How is it you don't have morning voice?" He spoke next to her ear.

She turned her head slightly. "Morning voice? What's that?"

He helped her shift around to face him so that they could talk more easily. He'd learned that much the night before. Without her hearing aids, Audrey had some hearing and did well, particularly when it was quiet, but when she could see the speaker, she did even better. Making love in the soft light of her bedside lamp had been wonderful, he thought. Who cared if it was practical too? "You know, when you're all tired, and your head is still half asleep, and your voice sounds like you just woke up. You sound like it's the middle of the day. How do you do that?"

He loved to hear her laugh. "I have no idea. I'm just me. I wake up, and I'm awake. I guess I don't do that middle ground stuff."

"Middle ground, huh?" He kissed her on the nose and then pulled her closer to him so that his lips were right beside her ear. "I wish I had a

lot more time for the middle ground, as you call it, but I think we both
need to get a move on. Do you have any coffee?"

"Are you kidding?" She sounded as if he'd just suggested that humans
walk on two feet. "Of course I have coffee, the good stuff, too. Why don't
you take the bathroom while I set it up?" He kissed her one more time
and reached for the clothes he'd tossed on the floor by the bed. He held
them in front of him as he moved toward the bathroom. Rod didn't want
her to think he had a one-track mind, after all. Once inside, he noticed
a fresh set of towels hanging on the back of the door, so he took the opportunity to take a quick shower. He might show up at work wearing the
same thing he had on the day before, but at least he wouldn't smell like
it. Now, if only she had a spare toothbrush, he'd be all set.

In just a few minutes, he was headed to the kitchen while Audrey slid
past and into the bathroom for her turn. He could hear the commode
flushing and then the sink and what sounded like someone brushing
their teeth. Finally, he heard the coffee maker ding that it was ready and
poured himself a mug. There was a new loaf of bread on the counter, so
he pulled out a couple of slices and slid them into the toaster.

When she emerged, he saluted her with the mug. "You're right. This
is excellent coffee. I may never leave!" She came up next to him and put
her arms around his neck.

"Stay as long as you like." He hoped that the coffee was masking the
worst of his morning breath as he pulled her close and kissed her again.
She pulled apart then and moved to open the refrigerator door.

"I hope it's okay. I made myself at home and put in some bread to
toast."

She emerged with a butter dish and what looked like a jar of homemade jam. He was definitely staying. "That's great, thanks. Here's some
butter and cherry jam my friend Sandy made while she could still get
around in her kitchen. That reminds me, I need to check my phone.
Give me a second."

She pushed the button to activate the phone, and a bright light flashed
briefly. Then she looked up. "Mom says Sandy's great but exhausted, and
one of the twins was having a little trouble at first but is doing better
now. Sandy says we can visit any time after nine this morning."

Rod sat down at one of the stools and took another sip of coffee just as the toaster popped. Audrey was bringing over a plate with his toast and putting two more pieces in for herself. She got out a second plate, and Rod held his out toward her. "Here, have one of these with me, and then we'll do the same with the next round."

Audrey poured herself a mug of coffee and then took turns with the butter and jam. She looked at Rod to see what he thought of the jam. "It's delicious, isn't it?"

"It's all good, the jam, the toast, the coffee, you. Now, if you happen to have a spare toothbrush, everything will be perfect."

"As a matter of fact, I do."

"Well then, perfect it is."

Forty-five minutes later, Rod was pulling away from Audrey's gym headed to the precinct. Her mother was going to pick her up from there once she finished, and then they were headed over to the hospital to see her friend and the new babies. The plan was that her mother would drop her at home, and then she'd call a car for the trip to and from the downtown hotel that evening. It was the best they could do for now. They would get together Saturday for lunch and talk about what other steps they could take. She'd called the landlord that morning, and while he'd agreed to update the keypad, it wasn't going to happen before next week. Rod wondered how open she'd be to staying at his place for a while. God, he'd have to clean it first. He and Simon had their work cut out for them this evening.

The area with the detectives' cubicles was reasonably quiet when he arrived. With opioid deaths on the rise, homicides in the city seemed to have fallen off, oddly enough, and their staff had been cut accordingly. He just hoped they'd keep Smitty's spot for him until he was able to return. For now, though, Rod didn't mind the quiet as he reviewed the notes he'd made so far and then began listing the questions he wanted to ask the staff at Mrs. Pelletier's home. He knew that the Airbnb rental was ending today, and he wanted to talk with the staff before the Pelletier children arrived and began taking over the house. Gabriel Perez hadn't been free when he called, but once Rod outlined the questions he was planning to ask, the young man had seemed satisfied. Rod knew he would call later if anything came up with his family.

Rod pulled up just before 9:00 and was pleased to see that there weren't any other cars on the long drive. He'd called ahead, and Mrs. Garcia met him at the door. "Thank you again for speaking with me, Mrs. Garcia. How are you all doing this morning?"

"We're good, Detective. Come on into the kitchen. My brother and sister-in-law are there as well. We've just finished our breakfast, but we do need to get to work soon."

He followed her down the hall to the back of the house and was pleased to see the other two seated at the small table as expected. Mrs. Garcia poured him a cup of coffee and gestured him into the chair at the head of the table before sitting down herself. "Thank you, that's very kind of you. I know you all have work to get to, but I wanted to ask just a few more questions if I may." They looked at him expectantly, so he continued. "First, I wondered if any of you had any new thoughts as to what might have happened the night Mrs. Pelletier fell, what might have woken her up, for example?"

The housekeeper, Valeria Perez, answered first. "We've talked about nothing else since it happened, but we haven't figured it out." She gestured to the man beside her. "My husband Ernesto has been out working around the house, and he's seen nothing out of place at all, nothing in the flower beds under the windows or in the walkways, nothing near any of the doors."

Ernesto spoke then, his accent slightly thicker than his wife's. "She's right. We keep trying to think of what happened, but we get nowhere."

"You were expecting her children for the weekend, right? So you were making up the beds, you said?"

"Sí, that's right," Claudia answered. "They were all coming for Mother's Day weekend to be with Mrs. Pelletier."

"What sort of an employer was she? Did you feel that you communicated with her well?"

Mrs. Perez answered this time. "Oh yes, her Spanish had a little bit of a French accent to it, but she was very fluent. We joked with her about it, but we understood each other very well."

"What would you say was her state of mind on Wednesday evening? Did it seem like she was looking forward to having her children home, or was there tension, worry maybe?"

"They were all having trouble." Mrs. Perez continued in a more somber tone. "She was worried about them all."

"Did she mention that her daughter might be coming to stay for a bit along with her granddaughter?"

"Yes," Mrs. Garcia answered. "We had picked out two rooms upstairs that were next to each other. She was hoping they would stay."

"And the sons? What did she have to say about them?"

Both women looked at each other and spoke at the same time. "Worried." Mrs. Garcia continued while the other woman nodded her agreement. "She was worried about both of them. She never liked having the older son so far away, especially since she heard about his divorce."

Rod thought about mentioning the alcoholism but decided against it. The man was sober now, and there was no need to share his past with them. "And the younger son? Did you or Mrs. Pelletier know about the scandal up in Buffalo?"

They looked around the table at each other, but no one seemed to have heard about it. Mrs. Perez finally responded. "We haven't heard anything, but she was looking forward to seeing all of her children, Detective. We knew them when they were growing up, and we were so worried for her daughter and granddaughter when the fires happened. We were watching them on TV with Mrs. Pelletier last summer."

"They were sweet children." Mrs. Perez added, and her husband was nodding his head in agreement. Rod thought he heard a car pulling up the driveway, so he tucked his notebook away and stood.

"Thank you very much, Mr. and Mrs. Perez, Mrs. Garcia. I appreciate you taking the time to talk with me. I'll let you get to your work now." The housekeeper led him to the door while her husband pushed in the chairs and began to carry the dishes to the sink. When she opened the front door, Arnaud Pelletier, Jr. was just reaching for the knob.

He jumped back when he caught sight of the detective, and Rod watched carefully for any signs of guilt or fear on the man's face, but he simply looked surprised. "Detective Rodriguez. Is something wrong?"

Rod tilted his head slightly as he looked at the man. He felt like making a sarcastic remark given that the something wrong was pretty damned obvious, but instead, he kept it to himself and tipped an imaginary hat.

"Just had a few more questions for your mother's staff." He nodded goodbye to them both and then headed to his car before the son could ask him anything else.

The drive back to the station took long enough that Rod found himself paging through one possible scenario after the other to see if anything fit. He pictured each of the grown children hiding on the stairs, giving their mother the fatal push, but none of the images seemed to resonate with him. He thought again of the staff and wondered about the undocumented husband out on the road somewhere between here and Florida. But there was no way something that brought publicity to the household would help any of the staff, and the group around the table this morning knew it. From everything he'd heard, the woman was a kind, intelligent employer who communicated well with her staff. The fact that their well-being was taken into consideration in the woman's will spoke volumes too.

He pulled into the lot behind his building with no more sense of what to do than when he'd left. He certainly hoped Audrey was having a more productive day than he was. He enjoyed picturing her with her friend's babies, so he sent her a quick text. *"Still on for lunch tomorrow?"* He received a response immediately and was happy to think that maybe she'd been watching for it. *"Everyone's good. Heading downtown soon. Lunch sounds great, will text you in the morning with the time."* He sent back an equally quick response and then went inside to write up the last of his notes. He thought he'd head over to the hospital afterward. If Smitty was up to talking, Rod wanted to get his take on everything before making a final decision.

31

In the morning, Adams watched as Audrey stepped outside in her gym clothes. He was already dressed and started toward the door when he saw the cop following her out and leading her to his car. Well, dammit, there was that chance all shot to hell. He went back into his kitchen and put together a sandwich while he thought about what to do next. He had the night off, so that was helpful. On Fridays, the club did twice the usual business and used their A-team of bouncers to work the doors and the floor. He'd seen the men before, and all three were large enough to subdue a crowd with their bare hands. Tensions were high since the shooting the week before, so he understood the need for the muscle.

It meant that he had an open morning waiting for her to come back. He had discovered an older desktop computer in the small second bedroom and, although it had been covered with dust, it seemed to work just fine. It wasn't any slower than the ones he'd gotten used to at the prison, so he knew how to wait. The first thing he started with was an Internet search for the little bitch. It didn't take too long before he was looking at her website. He didn't care about the photographs, figured they were nice enough for suckers who wanted to pay a fortune for that sort of shit, but the site had a calendar function that he zeroed in on. It didn't give any detailed information, but it did block out dates when she was unavailable. From what he could see, it looked like she might have something this weekend. That evening as well as all day on Sunday, were both marked in red.

He leaned back in his chair before standing up to look out the window at her place. There was no vantage point from where the computer was located, and he had been moving back and forth to the window all morning. It was starting to piss him off. Fine, he decided, he needed to stretch his legs anyway. He pulled on a dark sweatshirt that was old and faded and didn't have any sort of logo on it and added a pair of sunglasses. He carried the gun in back, tucked into his waistband, but he didn't think he would need it. He walked first to the end of the block past where the cop's car had been parked. Then he crossed at the corner and headed back toward her apartment building. With no one around, he quickly keyed in the code and went in to look around.

A set of mailboxes lined up near the door, and he looked over the nameplates and discovered hers. He ran his finger over it for a moment before looking around at the small lobby. There was nowhere to hide there, so he went on up to the second floor where her unit was. There were four on that floor, probably small and not nearly as nice as the one he was in, he thought. However, he liked that the hallway turned so that there was a recessed area just off the steps to the left of her section of hallway. The window let in a little bit of light, but there was only a single bulb hanging from the very top of the stairway, and the recess was shaded a bit by the landing itself. Well, this was looking easier than he thought it would be.

He stepped back into the recessed area and took a few practice strides toward her door before he heard another door close nearby. He left quickly and continued down the street for three more blocks before turning a corner and taking his time going back. He hadn't noticed a single person looking at him. The few people he met had their heads in their phones and were oblivious to the world around them. He thought what a total change it was from twenty years ago. The phones were handy sure, but it still seemed pretty stupid to him. Maybe it was just because he didn't have one himself. He knew they were used to trace people's locations all the time, and he wasn't taking any chances on that. He bought a couple of hotdogs from a vendor in the next block and headed back to the apartment. From the web page, he was assuming that there was some sort of event this evening. If she was working, he figured there was less of a chance that the cop would be coming home with her. Adams stood watching her apartment building as he finished his food and then turned on the TV. A few games would help pass the time. He hoped to see her come home before going out again, so he continued to keep a close watch.

Around three in the afternoon, just as he started to doze off, he saw a small station wagon pull up, and Audrey Markum got out. She leaned over to talk to the person through the window, and Adams thought he recognized the driver as her mother. Audrey waved and then headed into the building, but the car didn't move again until she was inside. Definitely a mother, dumb bitches. Always so overprotective, just like Lois had been with Toby. Turned the kid into a whiny mess.

He put Lois and the boy out of his mind and turned back to the game. It was nearly six-thirty when he saw her going out again, this time dressed up in nice black pants, a white shirt, and a patterned jacket. She was carrying a thick camera bag over her shoulder. Bingo, just as he predicted. He'd be waiting for her when she got back. Tonight he'd get back what she'd taken from him. He would take it nice and slow, enjoy himself for a change. He laughed as he started looking around the room, thinking how he would stage it. He thought maybe he'd set it up so that she could see her own apartment just like he did. Perhaps someone would even come there to check on her. Wouldn't that be fun?

32

The showers at the gym were tiny but private, and the water was hot. No one else seemed to be waiting for a turn, so Audrey took her time luxuriating in the heat. God, she had loved last night, she thought, and this morning as well. She had felt self-conscious at first since it had been so long since she'd dated anyone, but that feeling hadn't lasted. Not at all. Rod listened. That was her first thought. They took turns in their conversations without any of the impatience that Charlie used to bring to the table. She was happy too that Rod had liked her food, aside from the rice pudding, unfortunately. He seemed to feel about that the way she did about oysters. Probably it was a texture thing. She felt terrible that there hadn't been anything else to offer him, but he'd seemed happy enough, covering an extra roll in butter and then dragging it back and forth across both of their bowls.

They had taken their time talking about her fears and the strategies they could use to keep her safe, and he hadn't once made her feel silly or incompetent. She'd taken several self-defense classes over the years and shared with him what she knew about protecting herself. He had a few more suggestions that she appreciated as well. And then they had put it all aside.

She rinsed her hair one more time and took a second to stretch her arms up high before stepping out of the shower and drying off. Her mother wasn't due for another fifteen minutes, so she took her time getting dressed and dabbed on a touch of makeup. Next, she folded the sweaty clothes up into a neat bundle and put them into the bottom of the bag. Finally, she tucked her hearing aids into place and ran her fingers through her hair one more time before heading downstairs to wait for her mother.

When they arrived at the hospital, Audrey thought that Sandy looked exhausted and a little bit frightened as they walked in, but right on their heels was a nurse wheeling in a bassinet with a tiny baby in it. Audrey didn't even know that babies started out that small, and she was a little bit terrified herself, but the nurse parked the baby's bed next to the other one and then lifted the tiny form out and set her in Sandy's arms. "She's doing a lot better. I think she's ready for some mommy time."

"Really?" Sandy looked ecstatic as she cradled the tiny form against her. It was only then that she finally looked up and spotted Audrey and her mother. "You're here!" Sandy stage whispered, and Audrey gave her a quick one-armed hug before turning to hug her husband and her mother. All three of them looked tired, Audrey thought, but happy, nonetheless.

"So, do we have any names yet?" Audrey's mother asked Sandy.

"Trisha and Tisha." Sandy's husband announced, and Audrey was appalled, but then she heard Sandy laughing.

"Will you please stop saying that, you idiot? Someone's going to hear you and write that down if you're not careful." She turned then to Audrey and her mother. "They're named after our grandmothers. This one," she lifted the baby in her arms slightly, "this is Rose Marie Wilder-Jones, and that little cutie is Martha Ann."

"Oh, I like that. They're kind of old-fashioned names, aren't they?"

"Yes, I know it's long with the hyphen and all. We're not sure whether we're going to keep that or not."

"I love their names. I had a best friend growing up named Martha!" Audrey's mother added. "May I?" She gestured toward Martha and then picked her up carefully and brought her over near Audrey.

"She's so tiny!"

"And I'm still huge!" Sandy added, but her husband sat down on the bed beside her and took her free hand. There were tears in her friend's eyes, and Audrey loved how gentle his tone was.

"I'll stop calling them Trisha and Tisha if you'll give yourself a damn break. Look at what you did? I'm so proud of you. I don't even know what to say, but I do know I won't have anyone talking crap about my wife."

"Hear, hear," Sandy's mother added for good measure.

Audrey loved visiting with them. Sandy had never been shy, and it was fascinating to see how breastfeeding worked. They didn't know yet if she'd be able to keep up with the twin's needs, but she was doing her best for now. Finally, after they'd been fed, Oscar laid the babies side by side in the same bassinet. Within a few moments, Martha had found Rose's hand and was holding on to it, and soon both of them were asleep. It looked like magic as far as Audrey was concerned, nothing short of magic.

After their visit, Audrey and her mother ate lunch downstairs in the hospital coffee shop. The food wasn't great, but it didn't involve moving the car again, so that made it easy. Her mother was filled with stories about Audrey's birth and early infancy that she didn't think she'd heard before. It made her wonder if that day would ever come for her. They went back up after eating and visited for a bit longer before telling everyone a quick goodbye. Audrey's mother made a plan to come back the next day and help them swap cars so that Oscar and Sandy could drive the twins home in their new car seats.

Audrey was home in plenty of time to change clothes for the evening event and arrange all of her equipment. She was only going to take one camera and one camera bag with her, so many items had to be rearranged and consolidated. She also went through her purse and pulled out the things from it that she would need so that she could tuck them into the camera bag as well. She wasn't familiar with the room where the rehearsal dinner was being held, but she did know the hotel, so there was no need to leave super early. She called for a car about a half-hour before the event was scheduled to begin and was there in plenty of time.

This was going to be another easy wedding, Audrey thought, as she studied the group having cocktails and sharing stories. She learned that the couple had known each other for years and the families were familiar with each other as well. There seemed to be a lot of good-natured ribbing and storytelling going on, and that made it easy for Audrey to drift in and out, getting candid shots of the various groups. When it was nearly time to go into the meal, she had them gather for a few posed photos. Happy to have finished her task, Audrey was surprised when the best man ushered her into the dining area and indicated that a meal had been purchased for her as well. She hadn't intended to stay, but apparently, that hadn't been conveyed to the groom's family. She didn't want to insult anyone or have them waste the money on a meal, so she stowed her camera bag beneath the chair and took the offered seat. It was such a happy and festive group that it was easy to enjoy herself.

When the toasts began at the end of the meal, she stood and took a few more photos. She hoped to make her escape then, but the other end of the room had been cleared for dancing, and a band was beginning to play. Again, she was swept along with the group and found herself dancing with various members of the wedding party. It was friendly and easy-going, but the pounding bass quickly began to get to her, and after a half-hour of it, she retrieved her camera bag and said her goodbyes. She thought again that it was a good idea the wedding wasn't until Sunday morning, because this group would not be looking its best the next day.

As she stood in the lobby near the door waiting for her ride, she was relieved to be out of the range of the music finally. She had a headache that started at the top of her head and seemed to work its way down her spine. In the back of the car, once she'd confirmed her destination with the driver, she unhooked her aids and tucked them into the outer pocket of the bag. Her head continued to throb, but the quiet did offer a little bit of relief. She closed her eyes and was half asleep by the time they reached her building. She thanked the driver and took care of entering a quick tip for him on her phone before stepping out. She keyed in the code for the outer door and headed inside. She couldn't wait to take off the dressy sandals she was wearing and prop her feet up on the sofa. She was stuffed from dinner, but as she put her key into the lock, she was busy trying to remember if there was any ice cream left in her freezer. She spotted movement right behind her left ear just before two thick arms wrapped around her from behind.

33

When Rod walked into the hospital room, he had to check himself and make sure that the panic he felt at the sight of his partner didn't show in his face. Smitty was a fitness junkie who lifted weights and ran in races at least once a month. To see him now, his regular mocha coloring ashen from blood loss and pain, was shocking. True, he looked better than he had when Rod saw him right after the shooting, but he wished there had been more of a change. Smitty's head lay back against the pillow with his eyes closed. Rod hesitated in the doorway, concerned about waking him, but his wife Angela gestured for him to come in. At the sound of footsteps, Smitty opened his eyes and immediately looked a shade better. "Hey, how's it going?" He called out to Rod as he fumbled for the bed control. A whirring sound accompanied the slow rise of the bed until he was almost sitting upright.

Rod walked up to the bed and grasped his partner's hand in his, not letting it go for a long moment. "How are you, my friend? What's the word around here?" He looked from Smitty to Angela and back again when Smitty chose to answer.

"The word is 'it sucks.' Getting shot, being stuck in a hospital bed, having to eat Jell-O and pudding out of little cups, all of it."

"He's been whining about the damned pudding cups all day, Rod. Maybe you can get him to talk about something else for a change." Angela answered before leaning over the bed and kissing her husband. "I'm just going to get a cup of coffee. Do you want me to bring you something?"

Smitty shook his head and watched as his wife left the room. Rod thought he seemed to sag back against the pillow just a bit once she was out of sight. "So, pudding cups?"

Smitty laughed and then winced. "It seemed like a small topic, something innocuous to help her cope."

"Her?"

"Well, you know. Tell me what's been happening at the station. I was kind of hoping that the fuckers from the shootout were dead, but they're not, are they?"

Rod pulled a chair over beside the bed and sat facing his partner. "Nope, the cousin was in the ER for a few hours, but now they're all locked up."

"Shit, well, I guess that's okay. So what else is going on? What's up with the old woman with the money?"

"Well, if you're up to it, I thought I'd run it all down for you, see what you think. I've got to close it out, and I'm still on the pointy part of the fence about it."

A scratchy sounding speaker announced the end of visiting hours at the hospital at 8:30, and Rod stood to go. Smitty's wife Angela had given them a nice long chance to talk. It felt good to review his ideas with his partner, and it seemed as though Smitty liked having something else to think about. Rod was relieved to see him looking a little more like his usual self before he left.

Once he was home, Rod hooked Simon up to his leash. They took the longer route since the dog seemed to be feeling better. Sidewalks were busy with other people enjoying the spring evening, and Rod took his time, his thinking swinging around between the case, Smitty's health, and Audrey. At the first sign that Simon was having trouble keeping up, Rod found a bench and sat, giving the dog time to rest. Rod was kicking himself for not having brought some water along, but they weren't all that far away. Once the dog had rested, they ambled the rest of the way home. Rod reheated some pizza and put on the baseball game but was soon nodding off. Rather than spend the night on the couch, he shut off the set and headed to bed, figuring he'd check on the score in the morning. God, that seemed like an old man thing to do, but it couldn't be helped. At least he didn't have to admit it to anyone.

Sunlight began to fill his bedroom early, stirring Rod from a fitful night of sleep. Simon was still sacked out on the foot of the bed, so he climbed out carefully, not wanting to disturb the dog. After a trip to the bathroom where he deliberately did not turn on the light, Rod headed for the kitchen to make some coffee. He figured he'd need a big pot because it was time to write up the investigation and make a decision. As he fumbled with the jar of coffee beans, he thought again about Audrey and how quickly and easily she woke up in the morning. That just wasn't normal, he thought, shaking his head, at least not without a cup of coffee first. With the pot brewing, he went searching in his refrigerator for something to go with it. He was looking forward to an early lunch with Audrey, so he grabbed the milk and fixed himself a bowl of cereal. He figured that and the coffee should hold him while he worked. He ate the cereal standing over the sink and then left the empty bowl behind when the coffee maker chimed that it was done. Coffee in hand, he opened up his laptop and began to work.

He took a few minutes to read through the news headlines, checking on the baseball game first. The Pirates had lost by one in the ninth, so he was glad he hadn't bothered trying to stay up and watch it. He found a brief write-up about the dance club shooting and its aftermath. It reported that two officers were hospitalized, but neither one was still listed as critical. That was a huge relief. He closed up the news site and logged into the network for the police. As usual, Rod began by reading over what he'd written so far. Simon had woken up by then, so he clipped the leash on him and took him out for a morning walk. It was good to have the time to clear the rest of the morning fog out of his brain and review the case one more time before wrapping it up.

Once they were back home, and Simon had both food and water, the dog settled under the chair, and Rod got back to work. He thought back over his conversation with Smitty the night before and went through the file one more time, editing a few comments as he went along. Although Smitty had not spoken anymore with the Pelletier children, he seemed to trust Rod's gut instinct that told him they were neither capable enough nor guilt-ridden enough to have carried out a murder and hidden it so effectively. His talk with the staff the day before hadn't raised any suspicions either. He paged through the system until he located the form titled *"Death by Accident"* and began filling in the blanks. Finally, he attached the coroner's report and hit 'Save.' It was time to move on.

Once he'd hit the final key, Rod looked up at the clock and was surprised to see that it was after nine. He'd expected a call from Audrey by now, and he pulled out his phone to double-check. There was nothing. He punched in her number and prepared to wait, but it immediately went to voice mail. What the hell? She had her phone turned off? He left a brief voice message and followed it up with a text. "Ruby's *at 11:30?*" Then he went to take a shower.

Once he was out of the shower, dressed, and shaved, he checked the phone again. Nothing, no call or text, so he redialed the number. But the result was the same. Why in the world wouldn't she be taking calls? His thoughts immediately went to her talk about the man Adams having been at the market, and Rod wondered how long he needed to wait before it would be appropriate to panic. Given how he was starting to feel about her, he wasn't sure he could wait very long.

CHAPTER
34

When the arms came around her, Audrey dropped her weight into her hips the way she'd been taught and used the shifting momentum to flip her attacker over her head. In doing so, she lost her footing a bit and then discovered that her assailant's arm was tangled with the strap from her camera bag. Instinct told her to let go of the bag, but so much of her life was in it that in the nanosecond she paused, he was up again. This time he had a pistol in front of him. "Knock it off, bitch."

Audrey froze, seeing the hatred that filled his eyes when he spoke. He looked much as he had in the car passing by her so many years ago, and inside, just for a moment, she was that child again. She started to scream, but the pistol came up hard beside her head, and suddenly, everything went black.

It seemed as though she was only out for a moment. Audrey felt the floor beneath her knees and sensed Adams trying to lift her by her arm. She let her weight hang down as she fought to bring everything back into focus. "Stand up, Goddammit, or I'm going to shoot you right here." She caught a glimpse of his face then, and he saw that she was awake. Once she was standing, he pushed the weapon between her shoulder blades while holding her arm with his other hand. Instinctively, she had resettled her bag on her shoulder, and she walked ahead of him, holding it close to her side.

Adams had her pause at the outer doorway while he scanned the area around them. With the overhead light out and clouds moving in to cover the sky, it was difficult to see anything. He began pushing her through the doorway, and she tried to shuffle her feet and slow them down as she drew breath for another scream. But he sensed both of her strategies and leaned down next to her ear. "One move, and you're dead. Then I'll be back in the old neighborhood to take care of Mommy and Daddy, for good." Audrey quickly rethought her strategy and allowed him to walk her across the empty street. She was surprised that they didn't go far at all. Two doors down, he switched hands with the pistol and pulled out a set of keys. They were through the outer door and the inner one in just moments. The headache Audrey had been feeling earlier had now exploded, filling her head and body with pain. She sensed that her legs might give out once more just as he shoved her into a chair in the middle of a living/dining room area. The big screen on the far wall was showing a baseball game, and Audrey wished in that instant that Rod was beside her.

The chair that Audrey had been tossed into was wooden, a heavy, old-style desk chair that felt as if it weighed a ton. It barely shifted as she was thrown into it. Adams snatched the bag off her shoulder and threw it against the far wall as he leveled the pistol at her face one more time. He had picked up a section of nylon rope that was lying on the table and seemed to be weighing how to maneuver it and the gun at the same time. Audrey watched as he dropped the rope and brought his fist up in a punch that connected with a cracking sensation. Then all was black again.

As she came around, Audrey opened her eyes a fraction and tried to determine what inning the game was in, to gauge how much time might have passed while she was unconscious. But without her hearing aids, the sound of the television set was muffled and too hard to understand. It looked like the Padres and some other west coast team, so that didn't help at all. She looked around and saw the back of Adams' head where he appeared to be sitting on the sofa watching the TV. For some strange reason, that made her angrier than the punch. Fucking bastard, asshole sitting there watching the fucking TV while she was in agony.

She tried to think of more curse words to spew at him in her head, but her vocabulary seemed to be lacking, so she repeated to herself the few that she'd used already. Then she worked to steady her breathing, wondering what in the world she could do to escape. She tried to pull her hands from the rope, but they were bound tight, and pulling on it made her wrists, as well as her head and back, ache. She looked at her bag just out of reach and felt her shoulders sag. It was small comfort, but she was relieved to see that she was still wearing the clothes she'd had on and, other than them being torn from the fight in the hallway, they seemed to be intact. However, she could feel that there was blood drying on her face, and it was no longer possible to breathe through her nose. She tried to tip her chin down so that she could wipe some of the blood off on the shoulder of her jacket, but moving her head made everything worse, so she stopped. She looked down slowly at the front of her blouse, where blood was spattered and drying. Dammit, she loved this outfit, now look at it.

When the game went to a commercial, Adams stood and came back to stand in front of her. She pretended to be out still, but he saw through the ruse and barked at her. "Give it up, bitch. You're here, you're mine, and there's nothing you can do about it."

She opened her eyes and focused them on her attacker. "But why? Why am I here? I don't have any money. What do you want?"

He backhanded her hard across the mouth, splattering more blood and causing her bottom lip to begin swelling fast.

"Money? Do you think this is about money? I want my Goddamned twenty years back. I want my wife and my house back. You gonna give that shit to me? That's what this is all about. So you can just shut the fuck up while I finish watching this game. Then I'll decide what I'm going to do with you." He backhanded her once more, this time from the other direction, and Audrey was out again.

The next time she came to, it was dark. The television was off, and Adams was nowhere to be seen, although a slit of light was visible from the bottom of a door down the short hallway off to her left. Her arms and legs were numb where they were tied to the thick wood. She licked her lips carefully and discovered they were thick and cracked and tasted of blood. Inside her mouth, it felt as if two of her teeth were loose. She tried to shift her feet, edging them apart to see if she could slip out of the tight cord, but it gave very little, and she began looking around her once again. Surprisingly, Adams had drawn the inner curtain, but not the heavier ones, and, through the thin fabric, Audrey could see the outline of her own apartment. The light she always left on in the kitchen was burning brightly. It was hard knowing that both safety and comfort were so close by. She cried silently as she continued looking out the window and discovered that the earlier clouds seemed to be breaking up. A thin shaft of moonlight made its way in, shining onto the small table by the window. A week ago, it was full and bright, she remembered, and suddenly she knew what had awakened Mrs. Pelletier. Little good it would do anyone now.

Audrey watched for any other signs of light or movement outside, but there were none. The fear and pain continued to swell as she watched the thin strip of light go out, and Adams opened the door.

35

Adams stood in the bathroom staring at himself in the mirror over the sink. There was a bruise forming under his right eye where he'd hit the floor in the hallway outside her apartment door. Damn, who knew the bitch had that in her? Of course, it only threw him off for a moment, but it was still infuriating. His go-to move with Lois had always been to strangle her, or the kid for that matter, but he was unsure now, and he continued to stare into the mirror, letting his focus haze as he thought about what to do next.

It was possible to admit to himself that he hadn't thought this plan through to the end. He had enjoyed hitting her and watching her pass out and come to, especially with the crowd on the TV cheering. That was a nice touch, but he wasn't quite sure what he wanted to do next. He was way more interested in watching her suffer than he was in having her die. Maybe he could get her to do some begging like Lois used to. She would promise him anything when he had the upper hand, and he wondered what this bitch might offer in the same circumstances. Finally, he hit the light switch and headed back toward the darkened living room.

"Look at that cozy little place across the street. It's got a little night-light on just waiting for you to come home, doesn't it?" He got no response from her, so he slapped her across the face once again. "I said, doesn't it?"

Audrey held her head up to face him, but she still didn't speak. That made him even angrier, and he fastened his hands around her neck, squeezing and lifting up until she was gasping for air and her eyes had grown wild. Then, as she was just about to pass out, he let go and watched the blood rush back into her face as she coughed and choked, trying to draw air back in. He stepped back so that she couldn't spit on him. He wished he could see her face a little better, but he liked the way she could see her own place in the dim light, so he left the switch off and the heavy drape open. He walked to the window and stood looking out, waving the sheer fabric in his hand.

He figured he had two things to decide. The first was how to exact more pain and suffering and, therefore, begging. The second was when to kill her and how to dispose of the body. It occurred to him then that the apartment had been sublet using phony paperwork that could never be traced to him. So the easiest thing would be to wipe it down and then walk away. He could even leave her alive if he wanted to. The owner wasn't due back for over three weeks. He liked the thought of that, letting her starve and die within sight of her apartment while he walked away. He'd just have to find a way to keep her quiet. But he wanted to enjoy this for a while longer, and he realized he was tired. He'd been waiting in her hallway a long time. He looked at the fear on her face and circled her chair slowly. He yanked on the cords around her hands and then her feet, but they still felt secure. He wanted to gag her to keep her quiet, but that would have killed her quickly, given the state of her nose. There was no satisfaction in that. So he brought his pistol back out and held it against her cheek as he circled back around to face her.

"What I said before still goes. If you make one sound, my next stop is your folks' house in the old neighborhood. I know exactly where to find them." He studied her face for a moment longer and then left the room. He thought maybe he'd catch a little bit of sleep while he figured out what he wanted to do next.

36

Audrey was shocked that he would leave her there and just walk away. It looked as though a bedroom was just the other side of the bathroom, and the hallway filled with light as he entered it. She couldn't see anything more than the door before the light went out. Was he going to sleep? Her brain filled again with the few epithets that she knew, and she ranted and raved and called him every bad word she'd ever heard. But she did it silently. She believed him when he said he'd hurt her parents, and she didn't want to risk bringing any harm to them. She looked out the window and felt again how tightly her hands and feet were bound. She struggled to think what else she could try.

Her bag lay on its side against the far wall. She was surprised that Adams hadn't paid much attention to it. She worried about the state of her camera after the rough way it had been handled, but what she really wanted to get was her phone. She prayed it still had some power left. The chair she was tied to was heavy, but it wasn't attached to anything, so Audrey tried to move into a squatting position to see if she could lift it off the floor. It was awkward, and her quads started to burn, but it was possible. Her breath quickened, and she raised and shuffled a step to her right. She wasn't sure how much noise it made as she resettled the chair on the floor, but she didn't detect any movement from the bedroom. She could do this. She needed her phone if she was going to have any hope of surviving. Slow and steady, just like the tortoise, she thought. Be the tortoise.

There was no way to know what time it was or how long it had been since he'd brought her here. She thought that there might be a little bit of light coming into the sky, but it was hard to be sure. She began to follow a pattern, lift, shuffle two steps, rest, then repeat. It felt as though it was taking entirely too long, and each time she paused, she checked the hall and strained to listen for him. Finally, she was in front of her bag, but with her hands behind her, she didn't know how she would get into it. She'd worn nice sandals to the rehearsal dinner that she thought maybe she could toe off. Perhaps without them, she could wiggle free of the cord around her ankles. She hesitated a moment, not sure that she could get them back on. Oh well, she'd have to risk him noticing it, she decided. She struggled for a bit before she was able to drop the first sandal carefully to the floor. With a bit of a struggle, she managed to pull one foot out of the cord. She tried to pull the zipper tab with her toes, but it wouldn't budge. Once both sandals were off and both feet free, she used them to tug the whole bag closer and straighten it up slightly. She tried to pull the tab again, and this time it slid open. Now the side pocket gaped, and she could see her phone tucked just inside, but how could she get it into her hands?

She used one foot to pull the phone out slightly before using both feet to lift it out. There was a dining table and chairs not far from where the bag rested, and her chair teetered as she leaned back in it carefully and raised her feet to set the phone on the seat of the closest dining chair. The phone nearly slipped off onto the floor, but she quickly touched it back from the edge and then straightened her chair and rested. Her breath was coming out in small pants, and it felt as though her heart was racing. She strained to listen and thought that maybe she heard a sound from the back room. If only she had her aids in, she might have been able to tell. Without them, she had to rely on the light she'd seen, and so far, it hadn't come back on. She used her foot to resettle the bag and make it look like it had earlier. Then she slowly turned around and positioned herself in front of the chair with the phone on it. When she was as close as she could get, she reached out, the cord cutting into her wrists even more. She finally touched the edge of the phone. She forced herself to keep reaching despite the pain and was finally able to grab hold of it. Then the light in the back room turned on.

Audrey pushed and held the button to turn off the screen and then hoped she was swiping the correct way to power the phone down. She didn't want any of her alarms to go off, and she needed to save whatever battery it had left. A bright light appeared in the hallway suddenly, and she watched as Adams moved from the bedroom into the bathroom. She froze, expecting him to look into the room and see that she had moved. She held her breath, but he went into the bathroom without looking. She took one deep breath, resumed her squatting position, and pushing her sandals ahead of her, shuffled as quickly as she could back to where she'd started. She slid her feet back in between the cords and then slipped the sandals on the best she could. She tucked the phone into the back of her pants and pulled her blouse down over it as she worked to quiet her breathing. She was exhausted, and her wrists and legs now hurt along with her head, but a tiny hope had sparked inside her. She wasn't ready to give up yet.

37

Adams lay down on the bed on top of the covers and tried to think what his next step should be. He tried working through several scenarios, but he wasn't finding satisfaction in any of them. He closed his eyes and wished for just a few moments that he was back in the old neighborhood sleeping in his own bed. He drifted in and out of a light sleep imagining it, but he was kidding himself if he thought he'd find rest. Finally, he gave up and went into the bathroom, took a piss, and then stood looking into the mirror. Enough, he thought. This was a stupid idea. He needed to just get rid of her, get rid of her family, and then take off. He'd leave the state and start someplace new. It was time to settle the score and move on.

The first light of morning was coming into the room as he entered and saw the bitch sitting in the chair, looking all around her and then fastening her eyes on him. Something looked different, but he wasn't sure what it was. He studied her from a distance before coming closer and backhanding her across the face once more. It was satisfying to see her lips split once again, but she still didn't speak. He wrapped his hands around her throat once more and repeated the earlier motion, squeezing and lifting her off the chair.

"Nothing to say? Nothing you want to ask me? Beg me for? My wife and son were great beggars. You know that?" He raged, watching as she kept her now bulging eyes on him. Finally, when she was nearly passed out, he released her and waited while she coughed and choked once more. But even after that, she still said nothing. Well, fuck it. It was time for him to go. He went into the kitchen, came out with a plastic container of antiseptic wipes, pulled out two, and headed back into the bedroom. He found a duffle bag in the closet. It was empty except for a filthy old bandanna. That might prove useful, he thought and slipped it into his back pocket. He stashed his few belongings in the bag and then began wiping down every surface he felt he might have touched. He brought the duffle out, gathered his things from the bathroom, and repeated the process with two fresh wipes. Back in the dining area, he tossed the bag over by the door and went into the shallow kitchen, gathering up whatever food he thought he would take before wiping down the surfaces in there.

When he came out, he took the plastic bag of food he'd collected and dropped it into the duffle as well. He made sure that Audrey watched him as he took his time sanitizing the apartment and removing any traces of himself. He cleaned off the end tables and the remotes for the TV, then with more wipes, he cleaned the dining table and chairs. He took his time, relishing the fear that he saw growing on her face.

"Want to know what I'm doing?" He picked up her camera bag and tossed it onto the duffle too. "Probably get a pretty penny for that, I bet." He continued to tease her, but she said nothing, and he decided he'd had enough. As she watched, he pulled the bandanna out of his back pocket. It was dry and crusted with salt, but he picked the knot apart, opened it on his knee, and then refolded it until he had a long strip wider than her mouth. "Guess you're not going to use that mouth, huh, bitch? Well, we'll go see if mommy and daddy have anything more to say than you did." With his left hand, he wadded up a couple of wipes, and just as she started to scream, he smashed them against her lips and then pulled the bandanna tight over them before tying it around the back of her head. Her nose was still blocked, and he watched as her eyes grew wide and she grunted a muffled sound. But clearly, no air was getting in. She demonstrated surprising strength as she thrashed around trying to dislodge the gag, shocking him when she pulled her feet out of the cords and began to stand. Still tied to the chair, she stumbled toward him, but her hands were still lashed tight, and it wasn't long until her head slumped forward, and she fell back onto the chair. He waited for several minutes until he was sure she was gone and considered leaving her right where she was, but then he wondered if there might be prints left on the nylon. He needed to be sure, so he untied the cords, yanked the chair free, and tossed her body forward onto the floor. Then he wrapped the nylon around his hand and dropped it into the bag before wiping down the chair and placing it back by the small desk. He tied up the bag of trash he'd collected and slung the duffle over his shoulder. Locking the door behind him, he wiped that too. He tossed the bag of trash into a dumpster just up the block and headed to a car rental place that he'd located the day before. He hoped he'd find the mother home alone first, but either way, the parents were next on his list.

38

When he came out of the bedroom, Audrey felt that something had changed in Adams's demeanor. He stared at her hard at first, and she worried that he could tell she'd moved the chair. Then he began goading her, trying to get her to respond. He hit her and began choking her again. Her throat was screaming with pain as she gasped and coughed, trying to draw air back into her lungs. She wanted to scream and yell, but she knew she had no power other than her silence. If he was planning to kill her, Audrey thought, then there was no reason to chat about it first. She watched as he moved around the apartment slowly, wiping down every surface, returning everything to what she assumed was its original place. She wanted to cry when he took her camera bag and tossed it with his things, but she kept silent, grateful that she had managed to get her phone out of it first.

It looked as if he was finished with his cleaning, and her fear grew again. Finally, when he announced that he was going for her parents, she started to scream, but he shoved the acrid wipes at her mouth and then tied it shut. She fought to stand up and tried to hold onto the little bit of air that she had, but it was soon gone, and pain filled her head. Then once again, everything went black.

The first thing that she noticed was the floor beneath her cheek and the bright sunlight filling the room. She remembered wishing for the dawn and now panicked at how much time might have passed, before suddenly realizing that she was still alive. She had no memory of what had happened, but when she'd landed on the floor, the bandana had slid down her face, pulling the wipes away from her mouth just far enough that air was getting in. She started to move her hand to pull it off entirely and realized that her wrists were no longer tied together. Neither were her ankles. He had assumed she was dead. So had she.

With the bandanna off, Audrey slowly pulled herself up to a seated position and reached for her phone. It was warm from her skin, and she prayed it still had power as she held onto the button and waited for it to come to life. The low-power signal was on, so she quickly texted Rod, her fingers fumbling with the keys. "*Help.*" It rang almost immediately, but she promptly declined the call and instead texted, "*Can't hear.*"

"*Where are you?*" He texted in reply.

By this time, Audrey was dragging herself to her feet, stumbling with the pain and exhaustion but moving to the door and then out onto the sidewalk. When she was sure she could reach it, she paused to write. "*My apartment. Come quick!*" Then her hand dropped, and she forced herself to focus on keying in the code and getting to her apartment. She was barely standing, leaning on her door, when she realized she didn't have the keys. Tears poured down her face, but a flicker of light caught her eye, and she spotted them lying on the floor in the corner. She fell to her knees to pick them up and struggled with what little strength she had left to stand and insert them into the lock. She stumbled inside and turned to throw the deadbolt before she remembered that Rod was coming, or at least she hoped he was. Her parents were not reliable texters, but she didn't trust her hearing on the phone, so she sent them the message and hoped they would heed it. "*Look out for Adams in your neighborhood. Dangerous! Call police.*"

Audrey refused to give in to the fear that was washing over her and, instead, forced herself to stand and move again. She went into her bedroom and dug into her jewelry box for her old set of aids. She tried to remember to keep good batteries in them, and she was relieved to see that they had power when she turned them on. She was about to put them in when her hand brushed against the dried blood on her face. She set them down on the dresser and went into the bathroom.

She hadn't realized she was crying until she saw her face. Tracks of tears were dripping down across the crusts of blood. Her left eye was swollen and turning dark, her nose was crooked, and her lips were twice the size they should have been. She wanted to fall on the floor and just keep crying, but her parents' lives were at stake. She couldn't give up now. She grabbed a washcloth from under the sink and let the water run until it was almost too hot to touch. Then she wet the cloth and carefully began wiping away the worst of the blood. It hurt too much to touch her nose, so she left that area alone, cleaning up the rest of her face as best she could. Then she dried her hands and put in the aids just as the outer door buzzed open, and a knock sounded on her door. He didn't wait to come in.

When she saw the look in Rod's eyes, she wanted to cry and hide her face with embarrassment, but she needed him too much.

"Oh, my God, sit down." He pulled out his phone. "I'm calling an ambulance!"

Audrey tried to speak, but it hurt so much she only croaked out the response. "No!" then she grabbed a notepad off the table and began writing. "He's after my parents. Help them!"

"Give me the address." He began dialing as she wrote out the address. "Give me dispatch."

Once he'd told them the situation, Audrey was still not willing to go to the hospital. "Take me to them, please? I need to see them!" She wrote.

He moved past her and into the kitchen, where he rifled through the drawers until he found two dishtowels. She watched as he put a handful of ice into each of them and brought them to Audrey. It hurt too much to rest either one against her nose, so she held one to her eyebrow and the other to her mouth. She'd lost a sandal in her movement between the apartments, so she kicked off the other and began to rise to move toward her bedroom. Rod rested his hand on her shoulder to keep her from getting up.

"Let me. What do you need?"

Audrey sagged against the couch, set one of the dishtowels aside, and then pulled up her pad again. "Black sandals under the bed, a clean shirt I can button in front." He kissed the top of her head and went to get what she needed. He held each shoe as she put it on and then started to help with her soiled top. "I don't think I can get it over your head without hurting you."

Audrey mimed tearing it, and he kissed her again before ripping the bloodstained top apart and peeling it off of her. He retrieved the washcloth and a towel from the bathroom and helped to clean her up a little more before putting on the fresh shirt. "Thank you. I don't want to scare them any more than I have to." She squeaked out the few words, and Rod quickly brought her a glass of water. Then he returned to the kitchen, filled a water bottle, and grabbed a protein bar off the counter. He tucked everything into a backpack that was leaning against the table, then stood in front of her and held out his arms.

"Let's go, Scout. We'll make sure they're okay and then get you to the hospital."

Audrey nodded gently, but even that was painful, so she led the way out the door and down to the sidewalk. A cruiser pulled up outside for them, and they both climbed into the backseat. "Hit it." He told the driver, and the siren began as they pulled hastily out from the curb.

39

Adams couldn't remember the last time he'd driven a car and, at the rental lot, his lack of a current license was an issue immediately. But he figured, that early on a Saturday morning, the dumb bastard who was stuck opening the place would probably be open to a little extra incentive. Sure enough, he flashed a wad of cash, and the car was his. Once he was behind the wheel, he rolled down all of the windows and relished the feel of the air as it swept through the vehicle. Even better than the big TV, he thought. The sun had risen on a cloudless morning, and he took his time, admiring the look of the river in the growing light. He considered getting on the highway to make his trip quicker but then changed his mind. Instead, he wound his way through good and bad neighborhoods, watching as shopkeepers set out signs and tables, the city waking up to a spring Saturday. The smell of coffee and newly baked bread filled the air. He pulled over and bought himself some breakfast before returning to the car. He tucked the coffee cup into the holder and drove one-handed as he peeled down the greasy wrapper and ate the egg sandwich in quick bites before the yolk could escape to drip onto the rental car or his shirt. Once he finished, he crumpled the paper into a ball and tossed it out the window before reaching for his coffee.

He was surprised at how much he was enjoying the drive. After he passed through the denser parts of the city, the landscape widened out. Trees started to outnumber the houses, and he began to notice landmarks that had once been familiar to him, although sometimes the amount of new construction left him unsure about the accuracy of his memory. In twenty years, the suburbs around the city had changed, but then so had he. How had he ever imagined that he could be happy in one of these shitty developments? It seemed like there was an asshole out walking a dog on every sidewalk. What kind of a life was that?

He sipped his coffee and drove slowly around the streets that led into the neighborhood where he and Lois had lived, finally pulling over to the curb when he found their old house, now painted a hideous shade of green, its lawn littered with plastic toys. The front window had paper decorations stuck to it, and he thought about putting a bullet through it just for good measure. He set down the empty cup and picked up the gun from the seat next to him, feeling the weight of it in his hand, imagining the sound and the look of the picture window shattering. It might be worth it, he thought. He brought his hand up and aimed before setting the gun back down and pulling away. Maybe later. He drove slowly past the woods where he'd hidden Toby's body, but what had once been a fairly thick stand of trees had been whittled back until you could see right through them to the surrounding spread of new homes. There was even a paved path now leading through the stand.

He shook his head. Why couldn't people just leave shit alone, he wondered? He drove on, looking for the Markum house but lost his way for a moment as the streets he'd known had been added on to and redirected around the expanding neighborhood. Once he found his bearings again, he stopped two doors down from it and noted that both cars were in the open garage. The bitch's father, he'd forgotten his name, was pulling the cord to start a dirty, red mower. It jumped to life, the engine's roar breaking through the quiet of the morning, making Adams even more ready to end the entire family. He despised the fact that he'd ever had any connection to that kind of life. He raised the gun, aiming for the man's head as he mowed the line of grass along the front sidewalk. It was perfect. He figured he'd pop him first. The noise would be covered by the sound of the mower. Then he'd pull into the drive and go inside to take care of the mother.

40

Rod noticed that Simon was still sleeping under the table and thought again about how old the dog was getting. It was going to be so hard to lose him. There was a deep sense of melancholy forming as he stared at the phone. Maybe she just wasn't as interested in him as he was in her. What did they call this, ghosting?

As he was sliding his telephone out of sight, it vibrated with an incoming text. He was pleased to see the caller ID until he read it. "*Help.*" He tried calling right back, but there was no answer, and he saw then what she'd written. He texted back immediately and was in his car on the way to her apartment within minutes. He lucked into a spot on the curb and didn't bother to finesse the parking job. Instead, he ran up the stone steps, punched in the code he'd seen her use, and then raced for her door once the first one opened. He knocked but didn't bother waiting for an answer. He saw her immediately, standing near her sofa, hunched over slightly as she was putting in one of her hearing aids. When she turned toward him, he wanted to scream. She'd been beaten so severely he immediately starting dialing for an ambulance.

However, she was so emphatic in her response that he stopped and called dispatch instead to get someone headed to her parents' house and another car to come for them here. Then he set about getting her some ice and helping her dress to go out. He left the torn and bloodied shirt lying on the floor. Later they'd need it for evidence, but he didn't want her to have to think about it yet.

From the backseat, Rod could hear the back and forth on the radio and a report from the police dispatcher. Officers from Zone 6 were already approaching the area where her parents' home was located. Rod had sent all of the identifying information he had about Adams as well as an old arrest photo, but it would help if he had more.

"Do you know what he's driving?"

"No," Audrey answered.

"Probably a rental of some kind," the police officer who was driving added, and Rod agreed.

"What was he wearing? Length of his hair?"

He watched as Audrey closed her eyes briefly, and he was worried she might be losing consciousness, but then she spoke. It was raspy, but it was clear.

"He has hazel eyes, curly hair that's medium brown and comes down past his collar, but the last I saw him, he had on an old, red Phillies cap. He weighs at least forty more pounds more than he did in your photograph. He's got on a dark blue T-shirt with a medium blue plaid flannel shirt over it, blue jeans, and black running shoes. He knows that neighborhood, too. He used to live there, on Sycamore."

The policeman in front lifted his eyebrows at the detailed description and then called it into the station.

When he paused, Audrey added. "He also has a handgun. I don't know the make or model. It's black, about one and a half times the size of his hand."

The officer quickly added the information that Adams was armed.

Audrey had been trying to call her mother and father as soon as she was able to hear and speak a little better, but neither of them had responded. "What type of cars do your folks have?" Rod asked as she continued dialing them over and over again.

"My dad has a dark blue Hyundai sedan, and my mom has an old gray minivan." She looked up at Rod quickly. "She was going to the hospital today to help Sandy and her husband switch cars and bring the twins home."

"Try the hospital. See if she's there. Maybe your father is too."

Audrey tried Sandy's cell phone, but when it went straight to voice-mail, she dialed the hospital directly. Sandy and the twins had not been discharged yet, and the operator connected her to the room. When her mother answered the phone, Audrey's voice caught on a sob, and she handed it to Rod while she tried to regain control. "Mrs. Markum, this is Detective Rodriguez. I'm with your daughter Audrey. Can you tell me where your husband is? She's been trying to call him, and it's not going through."

"Is she all right? Can I talk to her?"

"Yes, to both, but first, how can we reach your husband?"

"When he dropped me off here, he said he was planning to mow the lawn this morning. So he would have left his phone in the house." Rod nodded so that the officer would send that information on as well. "Okay, Mrs. Markum, please remain there at the hospital. Audrey and I will come to you as soon as we can. She's been hurt . . ." Audrey yanked the phone back before he could finish and, with her poor, raspy throat, tried to calm her mother the best she could.

Rod hated that he was in the backseat rather than the driver's seat, but he held on to Audrey's hand and watched the streets fly by. They were making good time crossing a wide section of the city. Luckily, it was a Saturday. Once Audrey hung up, he pulled the water bottle out and pushed it into her hands. He thought her throat must hurt, given the way she gulped at the cold water. In the meantime, he peeled the wrapper down from the protein bar and handed it to her. She started to shake her head no, but he wouldn't take it back. "Just tiny little bites. It's okay. You need it." Audrey looked up at him with tears still filling her eyes, and he shifted to be closer to her in the seat. "It's going to be okay. They'll get him." He watched as she nibbled off the corner of the bar, but he noticed that when it reached her throat, she winced and pulled the wrapper back over it.

Their siren cut off suddenly, and Rod's head jerked up to look at the driver. The car was slowing as well. "What's going on?"

The radio crackled again, and the driver answered before turning to look over his shoulder at them. "There were shots fired at the house, and an ambulance is coming in." Just as he finished, the blaring sound of a siren grew deafening. Immediately after it passed, they took off again. Audrey was sitting, white with panic, both of her hands over her ears. It felt like an eternity, but within just a few minutes, they had caught up and were pulling over to the curb behind the ambulance. Its doors were open, and a gurney was being pulled out and yanked up to standard height.

"Wait here, and I'll find out what's happened." Audrey already had her belt off and was reaching for a door handle that wasn't there. The driver was around to Rod's side quickly, though, and was pulling his door open. Rod held his hand out in front of him and begged Audrey to wait. "Please, one minute, that's all I'm asking. I want to be sure it's safe." He saw her eyes flare in frustration and anger, but she paused. He closed the door gently and walked to where their driver was speaking with one of the other cops. "Rod Rodriguez." He stuck out his hand.

"John Chao."

"What's the story?" Rod gestured behind him to where Audrey's face was pressed up to the window. "She's hurt and panicked, and I don't think I can keep her in the car much longer."

Chao spoke into his radio for a moment and then turned back to Rod. "Scene is secured. The father is standing in the garage. He's not hurt."

"And Adams? Dead, I hope."

"Nope shot, but he'll make it. The other black and white unit spotted Adams parked in the neighborhood, and we boxed him in. He had his gun pulled out and took a shot at my partner, but the other team got him. The ambulance is for him." He jerked his thumb to where a body matching the description Audrey had given was being loaded onto a gurney and handcuffed into place. The man was screaming and struggling, but an oxygen mask quickly silenced him. As soon as he was secured, Rod went back for Audrey.

As they walked past, he saw Adams trying to stare Audrey down, but with true satisfaction, Rod noticed that she only had eyes for her dad and was in his arms within seconds. Once the gurney was loaded into the ambulance, Rod stepped over to the second EMT and asked her to follow him up to the garage to look at Audrey. She didn't want to let go of her father, now that she knew he was safe, so Rod gestured for him to bring her over to the porch so that she could sit down. Rod thought she looked as though she was ready to pass out again. He took off his jacket and laid it behind her so that the EMT could lay her back and examine her more carefully. As they took over, Mr. Markum released Audrey's hand and stepped forward.

"Who are you? What happened to her?"

"Mr. Markum, I'm Detective Rod Rodriguez. I haven't gotten the whole story out of Audrey yet myself. When I got to her, she was in a blind panic because Adams said he was coming for you and your wife."

"My wife?" He started, but Rod responded quickly to ease his fears.

"She's fine. Audrey talked to her at the hospital. We told her we'd meet her there."

Rod noticed then that the EMT was easing Audrey back up into a seated position, so he and her father approached. "She needs to go to the hospital. She has a concussion as well as a broken nose, and I want an ophthalmologist to look at her eye. I think it's fine, but we need to be sure." The woman jerked her thumb toward the ambulance. "She's not going to want to ride with that lowlife."

"I'll take her." Rod and Audrey's father spoke at the same time.

Audrey looked at them both. "Rod, you don't have a car here, and I'd rather not ride in any more police cars. Dad, will you drive me?"

"Of course." He dashed inside to collect his keys. Rod was feeling a little down until Audrey turned her battered face to him and asked. "Will you come with us? Can I give my statement, or whatever I have to do, to you?"

"Of course. Let me go tell our ride what's up." He had started back toward the car when Audrey wheezed out his name.

"Rod."

He turned back to face her.

"Can you find my camera bag? Could I have it? He took it with him, and I need it."

"I'll go and check. Hang on one second."

Rod worked his way around to the other side of the scene, where two uniformed officers were looking at the rental car. In the back seat was an open duffle bag and on top of it was what looked to be a camera bag.

He spoke to the nearest officer as he pointed inside the car. "That's the victim's bag there on top. Could I sign for it here and let her take it with her to the hospital? You could look through it first if need be."

The officer pulled out a stylus for the notebook he was using, made an entry, and then handed the stylus to Rod. "We already had a look-see, and it's fine. We're going to take the car and his stuff in, but I don't see why she shouldn't have her bag back."

His partner handed the bag to Rod. "Nice description we got over the radio, by the way. Made him as soon as we got into the neighborhood."

Rod grinned. "That's Scout for you. She's got quite an eye for detail." He gave a mock salute and then went to meet Audrey and her dad.

CHAPTER

41

By three o'clock in the afternoon, Audrey was lying on a hospital bed, still dressed in her spattered clothes and ready to go home. She'd been interviewed and photographed by Rod and another detective, her injuries carefully cataloged and recorded before she was treated. Then the eye doctor had examined her and pronounced her eyesight to be fine, after which they set her nose in a quick but painful procedure. Although the area around her eye was continuing to darken, the swelling in her lips was diminishing, and fresh ointment had been applied to the cracks. Her neck and throat still throbbed from the strangling, and the headache was blazing as well, but the doctor told her he thought it would improve overnight. Hence, the argument with her parents and Rod.

"He said it would get better tonight." Audrey was trying to convince everyone that she would be able to carry through with her job photographing a wedding the next day. She'd had a long conversation with the bride and groom, as well as the bride's mother. They all understood and were upset by Audrey's news, and they listened when she suggested that a friend of hers take over the wedding, given how bad Audrey looked. One after the other, though, insisted that they didn't care a whit for how she looked. They just wanted to know if she felt up to doing it or not. Of course, if they had to go with a substitute, they would, but it was clear that they would prefer Audrey.

More than anything, Audrey wanted things to go back to normal. She knew it would be a while before that happened, but doing her job was part of what made her feel normal. Her parents wouldn't hear of it, though. She looked at Rod and offered him a crooked smile. Then he stepped forward.

"How about this? I'll take Audrey to the wedding and keep a close eye on her, and in the meantime, I'll see that she rests and takes care of herself." Then he looked toward Audrey. "And if I see that's it's turning out to be too much for her, I'll call in the other photographer myself."

"She said she was willing to stand by in case I need her," Audrey added.

Audrey's mother sat beside her father on the plastic bench opposite the hospital bed. She was so grateful to have both of them there in front of her, but they were not buying this plan until Rod offered the kicker.

"Once the wedding's over, we're coming back to your place, and Audrey is going to stay there for a minimum of three days."

"What?"

"Great!"

Audrey and her parents all answered at the same time, and Rod began laughing.

"You three are quite a set." The nurse came in to drop off the final instructions that would allow Audrey to be discharged. She was sorry she hadn't had a chance to see Sandy one more time before they left, but if she were coming home for a little bit, they'd catch up soon. Reluctantly, her mother and father drove Audrey and Rod to her apartment in the city. There was a ticket on Rod's windshield, but she knew he'd deal with that easily enough. She leaned over the seat carefully to give her father and mother each a small hug.

"I'll see you tomorrow evening."

"All right, Audie. Rod, take good care of our girl, now. We'll expect you to stay for dinner tomorrow night as well." Her father answered.

Audrey looked up at the steps as the car pulled away and wondered if she had the strength to climb them or not. She'd done a bit of bluffing in the hospital to try and calm her parents' fears.

"Want me to pick you up?" Rod leaned over and gave her a gentle kiss on her cheek.

"No, but I will happily lean on you. I'm more tired than hurt at this point.

"Okay, leaning it is." He reached his arm around her shoulder and took her closer arm in his. "We can do this together, Scout."

Once inside, Rod deposited her on the sofa and then stood looking at her. "What?" She asked.

"You were putting on a show for your folks, weren't you?"

"How can you tell?"

"To be honest, you still look like you were run over by a bus. What do you need the most? How can I help?"

She leaned back and closed her eyes for a few moments as her thoughts tumbled, and she tried to restore some order to her thinking. Then, finally, she opened her eyes and studied the man in front of her. "First of all, I want to say thank you for everything." He leaned in to kiss her gently on the forehead before standing back up.

"No need."

"I know that I want to get cleaned up. They didn't do much of that at the hospital, but I'm really worried about my camera and the photos I took before this started. I need to see if they survived."

"Okay, how about this? I'll make a quick run home to let Simon out and make sure my neighbor can take care of him in the morning. After that, I'll grab some clothes for tomorrow and then pick us up some food. Will you be all right for about an hour? I can wait if you'd rather."

Audrey sat up a little straighter. "I'll be fine. If you hand me the camera bag and my laptop, I'll sit right here and work. I won't even get up."

Rod gathered the items she needed, retrieved a lap desk from her bedroom, and helped her to arrange everything within easy reach. He pocketed the extra key she'd given him so that he could lock the door and she wouldn't have to get up. Then he refilled her water bottle and set it down on the end table to her right. "Is that everything?"

"Yep, I'm good. Thank you so much."

"Okay." He pointed to the end table. "Your phone is right there, on the charger, so call or text me if you think of anything else that you need."

"Will do." Audrey watched as he waved his hand and carefully closed the door, locking it behind him.

With an eagerness that helped to distract from some of the pain, Audrey pulled the camera out of her bag and began checking it over. It looked to be intact. She held her breath as she hooked it to the laptop and waited for the download to begin. Once it did, she leaned back and took deep breaths in and out until it felt as if her shoulders were finally back down where they should be. She took a drink of water and heard the ice cubes clink, and marveled again at how thoughtful and kind Rod was being. She knew she was starting to fall for him, but it worried her as she tried to parse out the recent events. How much of it was him, and how much of it was due to the circumstances? But as she began to look through her photographs, she put those thoughts aside. She didn't have enough energy to think about more than one thing at a time.

Rod tossed the parking ticket onto the passenger seat and headed for home. He called his neighbor Mrs. Stefanyk, on his way over and was glad to hear that she would be happy to take care of Simon for him. She often helped out when his shifts ran long, and he appreciated the way she doted on his old friend. Once he was home, Rod took a few seconds to talk to Simon and rub his ears and belly before taking him for a short walk in the nearby park. When they returned, he packed up some of Simon's kibble and his bed and took him next door. Then he returned and scanned his closet, looking for something nice enough to wear to a wedding. He discovered his suit still in its dry-cleaning bag hanging on the back of the door. He grabbed up some more casual clothes as well and threw everything into a wide-mouthed gym bag. It already had a supply of toiletries, but he had to go looking under his bathroom sink for a spare razor and shaving cream. When he spotted the box that his sister had left behind, he grinned and tossed that in too.

"Hey, fifty-eight minutes. How's that for precision?" He was relieved to find Audrey right where he'd left her. She still looked awful, as well as tired, but he was so relieved that she was safe, he looked past it all. "Guess what my sister left behind the other weekend." Rod held up his find.

"Bath bombs? You have bath bombs?" Audrey laughed, and Rod thought it sounded miraculous.

"Yes, indeed I do. You know what these things are? I'd never heard of them."

"I love them, actually, but I don't keep them around."

Rod dropped his things by the bedroom door and hung the suit on a nearby hook. Then he carried the bags of food over to the kitchen counter. "I got a variety for you to pick from, but there's no hurry."

He watched as Audrey closed the lid on her laptop and set it on the sofa beside her camera bag before standing up slowly. He wanted to rush over and help but thought she would probably prefer to do it all by herself. When she got closer to the kitchen, he held his hands, palms up, like a scale he was balancing. "So what would you like first, food or bath?"

"Bath, I think, then food. But.."

"What is it?"

"I still feel a little wobbly. I'm embarrassed to ask, but could you help me in and out of the tub? I don't want to fall after all of this."

Rod stepped forward and pulled her gently toward him. "Why in God's name should you be embarrassed?" He took her hand and asked. "Okay, how hot do you like the water?"

She went with him into the bathroom to get the water started and then into her bedroom to pick out some fresh clothes. When she returned with a soft nightshirt, underpants, and an old pair of sweatpants, he was relieved. She wasn't trying to hide the pain anymore, and that gave him a good feeling. He liked that she was trusting him with all of this. Whatever had made him think she was ghosting him? He looked up at her before dropping in the bath bomb. "Ready? My nephew likes a nice drumroll with it."

Audrey didn't need the drumroll, but she did need help getting out of the battered clothes and into the deep tub. Once she settled in among the bubbles, he put her towel on the floor where she could reach it and then started to leave. "I'm just going to leave the door ajar so that I can hear you. When you're done, let me know, and I'll come help you get out." He pointed his finger at her with mock severity. "Do not get out without me. Are we clear?"

"Yes, Mom. We're clear!" Rod pulled the door halfway and went to the kitchen to begin sorting out some dinner. When she was ready, they reversed the process, but she was starting to shiver by the time they'd finished.

"Wait here." Rod found a zip-up hoodie and a pair of thick ribbed socks and brought them back to her. They heard her phone ringing as they emerged from the bathroom, so Rod handed it to her and settled her on the high stool.

"Hi, Mom." She answered, calming her mother's fears again and reciting how she'd been taking care of herself. Rod kept quiet as he set about warming the food and spreading it out, but he couldn't help but notice that she left out any mention of his help with the bath. That suited him just fine, especially since he'd be seeing her folks the next day.

Once she'd hung up, Rod held his arm out with a flourish. "Madam, your buffet awaits!"

As they finished their dinner, Rod could see that Audrey was flagging once again. "Come on, let's get you into bed. You're about to fall off that stool." After a few minutes, she emerged from the bathroom. "You okay?"

"This sucks, you know. I look like a total freak, and I can't even brush my teeth without it hurting." Rod was worried that she might break down entirely, but instead, she raised her chin and walked toward him. He held her to him again and admired the steel that held her together. Once she was tucked in, he lay down on top of the covers next to her. He held onto her hand and began telling her a story about a trip he and Simon had made to the beach. A third of the way into it, she was asleep. Once he was sure she was out, he slid off the bed, pulled the door nearly shut, and went back out into the living room.

He went to sit on the far end of the sofa where he could hear her, but he thought his calls wouldn't carry in to disturb her. He was moving her camera bag out of the way when he noticed the hearing aids in the open pocket. He remembered what Audrey had said about them being rechargeable and got up to see if he could find the base. It was resting on the windowsill behind the dinette table, so he set them into place and plugged it in. Then, he got a glass of water from the kitchen and settled into work. He had a number of calls to return, beginning with Smitty's.

When Audrey's phone lit up, he traded texts with her parents and her friend Sandy, assuring everyone that she had eaten and was now sleeping. Then he set both phones to 'do not disturb' and turned out the lights. For a moment, he stood in the bedroom doorway checking on Audrey. God, that fucker had done a number on her. He wanted to strangle the man with his bare hands. Instead, he went around to pull her blanket up and kiss her on the forehead. Then he left the door ajar again and stretched out on the sofa. For a long time, he lay staring up at the ceiling, experiencing everything over and over, but finally, sleep found him as well.

43

"Oh, my God, what in the world was I thinking?" Audrey stood in front of her bathroom mirror in the morning, staring at what had become of her face. Her left eye was less swollen now, but it was officially black with ugly green and yellow smears added to it. One edge of the tape on her nose was trying to come loose. Her lips were still twice the size they should be, but at least her teeth didn't feel loose anymore. She brushed her hair for whatever good that would do and came on out to the living room. Rod was back behind her kitchen counter again, and he looked up with a grin when she entered.

"Scout, it's good to see you!" He gestured with a wooden spoon but then quickly pulled it back over the pot of oatmeal. "Oops, how are you doing?"

Audrey came around the kitchen counter and put her arms around his waist as he stood stirring the bubbling pot. "I'm better." She finally answered. She went to the camera bag looking for her better hearing aids, but they weren't there. She looked around the bag but then caught sight of Rod pointing toward the windowsill. Of course, they were on the charger just where she needed them to be. He was a wonder, she thought, as she settled them into place and went to eat breakfast. She'd managed only a few bites out of the spread Rod had offered last night, but now she was starving. She finished one bowl of oatmeal and then, like Oliver Twist, asked for more. With that and two cups of coffee, she was feeling worlds better.

"Okay, Scout, so what do you think about this wedding? Are you a go or no?"

"Oh Rod, I look so terrible. I'm really thinking about canceling."

"That's not a reason, and you know it. I heard you on the phone with them yesterday, and I know that's not the issue. The question is can you do the job, not *how* you'll look doing it."

"You're right. Okay, let me get my camera." Audrey gathered what she needed and began taking a few shots around the apartment. "Rod, do you know if the hospital gave me any extra tape when they sent me home?"

He went immediately to the plastic bag with the hospital logo on it and pulled out a partial roll of surgical tape. Once they had her nose re-taped, she tested her camera again before sitting down on the couch. "I don't think I have the energy that I normally would, so I'm going to text the bride and see if they're okay with my skipping the brunch and just doing the wedding." The bride answered quickly, and Audrey leaned back with relief. "Are you sure you don't mind going with me to this? I know a fair number of people who hate weddings and wedding photography especially."

He shrugged. "I'm not going to a wedding. I'm going to help you. What time do we need to be there?" Together they calculated the time needed to prepare and drive to the downtown venue. "I talked to one of the guys handling Adams's case, and he'd like to come by and interview you again. Are you feeling up to it? He said he only wanted a half hour or so."

"Of course, but could you help wash my hair first?" He went to fetch the shampoo, and they were in business. After they finished, she stood wrapping the towel around her head. She turned to Rod again. "Hey, I know I just keep asking for things, but could you do me another favor, not right now, but later?"

"Sure, what's that?"

"Could you teach me how to swear?"

Rod looked dumbfounded. "Teach you to swear?"

"Yeah, when I was tied up, Adams kept wanting me to beg for my life or something, but I didn't want to give him the satisfaction, so I stayed silent. But," she touched her head with her free hand. "Inside my head, I was screaming at him, and I realized I have a really limited vocabulary in that area. I need to learn some other phrases, some really vile ones. I only know a few words like . . ."

He put up his hand. "Okay, I'm going to stop you right there. I get it. What we need to do is sign you up for Cussing 101 with Smitty once he's out of the hospital. He still comes up with phrases I haven't heard before. He was in the army, and he claims they teach it in basic training."

"Excellent! I want to learn some especially pithy ones!" She closed her hands into fists to emphasize the point.

"Pithy, got it. I'll be sure and let Smitty know." He was shaking his head as Audrey began humming a tune and moved back to the bathroom. When the officer arrived, Rod pulled out a chair for him and then sat beside Audrey on the sofa.

"First off, how are you feeling this morning, Ms. Markum?"

"It's Audrey, please, and I'm feeling better. Thank you for asking."

"I know you went through everything with us yesterday at the hospital, but I'd like to hear it all again if I could, now that you're feeling better. Could you start from the beginning? You were at a hotel, is that right?"

As he asked the question, Audrey worked her way through the events. Then she described waking up flat on the floor in the bright light of morning.

"So, he was cleaning up behind himself?"

"Yes." She described him shoving the wipes into her mouth and then tying the bandanna on her.

The officer looked from her face to Rod's before speaking to her again. "So, when he untied you and tossed you to the floor, he thought you were dead, correct?"

Audrey took her time before answering him. "I think so. I mean, I *was* almost dead. With my nose broken and my mouth covered, I couldn't get any air in at all. If the fall hadn't dislodged the bandanna, I'd have suffocated for sure."

Audrey squeezed Rod's hand tighter as the officer finished his questioning and then prepared to leave. "Thank you again, Ms. Markum. We'll be in touch if we need you for anything. Listen, it's been driving me crazy where I've seen you before, but I just realized. You've been taking photos for the police department, haven't you?"

Audrey led him to the door and shook his hand. "Yes, but I must say, I'd much rather film other people's crime scenes than participate in my own!"

"I hear that!" He left, and Audrey went to the couch and stood in front of Rod.

"If I sit down again, I may never get back up." She held out a hand as though she would pull him up. He got the message and stood in front of her, his arms open wide. She walked into his embrace and held on as long as she could. Definitely, she was definitely falling for this guy.

Audrey kicked off her shoes as she walked in after the wedding. She had pulled it off. She was proud of herself but could admit to the exhaustion now pouring over her. She collapsed onto the sofa and looked up at Rod. "I can't move at all. Everything aches. Places I didn't know I have ache."

Rod leaned in to kiss her before settling beside her and cradling her hand in his. "You were amazing, Scout. I can't believe how you held up after everything that happened."

"Do I still have to go to my parents'?"

"Yes, you do. They need to see you, and you need to be pampered. Besides, Simon's probably watching the door for me."

"You could bring him over here." She offered, but Rod just shook his head.

"Nope, not with your allergies and not with your parents watching their door for you."

Soon they were in his car heading west, retracing their route from the day before, but this time at a more leisurely pace. Audrey was tired, but her thinking was clear, and she had to know. "Rod, are we still going to see each other after all of this is over?"

She held her breath, waiting for his response. "Scout, I was in a panic when I hadn't heard from you for two hours. And that wasn't because you were hurt. I had no idea about that. It was because I'm crazy about you. Can't you tell?"

Audrey let her breath out and wanted to shout with the sheer joy of hearing that. But she reached for his hand instead and held on tight. "I am so glad to hear you say that. I'm pretty crazy about you, too. I mean, I may be a little crazy in general right now after everything that's happened, but yeah, I feel the same way. Oh hey, what did you end up deciding about the Pelletier case?"

"I talked it over with Smitty at the hospital, and he agreed with me, so we declared it an accident. I made a bunch of calls after you went to sleep last night and talked with the older son, Arnaud. They were all having dinner at their mother's house, so he put me on speaker. They were relieved, of course, and all three of them plan to stay at the house for a while. It sounded like they're planning to help each other out."

"I like that. It sounds hopeful." A ray of light caught Audrey's eye, and she turned to him quickly. "I forgot to tell you. I think I know what might have woken Mrs. Pelletier up."

"Really?"

"I think it was the moon."

EPILOGUE

The pain was excruciating, and then it was gone. She had no idea what to make of it. She seemed to be sprawled on the floor of the foyer, her dressing gown in disarray, a slipper tossed to the side. Then she felt a hand touch her shoulder before pulling back, still outstretched, to help her up. She stood, feeling lighter and younger all at once. She felt her hair rising gently and forming itself into a French twist, dark brown wisps floating just by her cheek. The color of her dressing gown deepened until she was draped in a green, fitted sheath, the pendant of a gold necklace falling gently between her breasts. Finally, she could see him as he continued to hold out his hand.

"Come, let's dance."

ABOUT THE AUTHOR

LINDA COTTON JEFFRIES grew up in Carlisle, Pennsylvania. She attended the University of North Carolina at Chapel Hill and taught special education for over thirty years. Her novels, *We Thought We Knew You* and *Who We Might Be*, were published recently by Fifth Avenue Press in Ann Arbor, Michigan. Strong women, suspense, and romance are the elements she most enjoy writing about!

www.LindaCottonJeffries.com